Their brief heated meeting one fateful night had singed itself into their minds. Not knowing of the other's identity, but unable to forget, had sealed their fate. The fire smoldered quietly in each of them as they tried to move on with their lives.

Eric Stiles was in the middle of chaos, searching for a killer.

Hunted by an obsessed psychopath, Rebecca Gailen was trying to be strong.

The world stopped for a moment as they looked up and saw the other standing just feet away.

His heart lurched, her armor shattered and the world started again as Eric's brother, Charlie, appeared to take her hand.

Family loyalty isn't a choice. When Rebecca's stalker rages out of control, Eric's decision haunts him and he struggles to stay away. Can he remain loyal to his brother, even if it means abandoning Rebecca when she may need him the most?

Serenity Lost
Copyright © 2019 Amy Romine
ISBN: 978-1-4874-2467-1
Cover art by Martine Jardin

Published by eXtasy Books Inc or
Devine Destinies, an imprint of eXtasy Books Inc

Look for us online at:
www.eXtasybooks.com or www.devinedestinies.com

Serenity Lost
Trust Me, Book 1

By

Amy Romine

DEDICATION

My husband, Robert, our three children and my extended family. To Brenda, my Donna, Sean, the man with the knowledge, and finally my professional family whose constant support will never be forgotten.

Chapter One

The warmth pooled against his hand until it overflowed between his fingers like a piece of silk. He pulled her closer, the suppleness of her back crashing against his chest. Her lungs spit moist air as they emptied. Her body writhed against him as he grew erect in need.

She was such a subtle creature, sheltered and innocent. Even her screams were celibate in torment. His fingertips caressed her temple. He kept her cheek pressed against his as if in an old Hollywood romance. It was the sway of her body that first enticed him. The way her hips spoke to him in a languid sultry voice.

He got her attention the way he had with all the others, money. He lavished it upon her, until she was so intoxicated that she fell onto the satin overlay, anxious for his calloused hands to roam her body. He enjoyed in her delights, as much as he had in the others before her.

He inhaled the scent wafting from her light hair as it fell across her shoulders. She smelled of sweet orange and mango. The drugs had taken effect, and she laid in a quiet apprehension. He kept a steady hand as the blade caressed the expanse of her neck. He looked for an area with the most longing and stopped. He teased her with a feather twist before he applied the exact amount of pressure to birth that single tiny bud. The air escaped him as it ballooned and then dropped. Trailing a stained path down her neck before curving and twisting to her collarbone where it rested.

He caressed his way across her abdomen, leaving a trail of

succulent sticky warmth as he went. He pressed the blade into her forearm and with a quick slice of pressure, he released the blood contained beneath.

His eyes opened to the glory of crimson beneath his hands. It embraced her, curving against her and it called to him. He heard that sweet siren so long ago. Its melody filled him like no other, and he swayed with her to the music of his mind.

He turned her within his embrace before he laid her on the black satin sheets. Her amber eyes had gone dim, but she was still stunning with her hair sprayed against the pillows. The rich pattern of crimson that poured over her white dress and ivory skin called to him. He leaned over with a gentle touch to her lips.

A final farewell in their bittersweet romance.

The hardened plastic and metal shook beneath his feet as the monstrous expanse hurdled down the street. The stench, a mixture of stale alcohol, cigarettes, sweat, and urine, was suffocating. He took a seat in the left corner, willing his senses to replay the orange mango he'd just savored.

His back arched in the bus seat as his mind fixated on the first pearl. The first tear of crimson shed from her glorious body. He was always fascinated to watch how it would roll. The path it would take down the neck.

He giggled in joy and he saw a few eyes pass over him as the shaking vehicle continued to race forth. He ignored their glances, knowing that they would never experience such ecstasy as to warrant that particular titter.

The bus slowed and stopped. He rose and exited onto the street. The air was thick and cool, the rain had stopped. Their home was such a dreary place. He longed for sunshine. He walked several blocks and then turned into a residential area.

He heard the closing of a car door. He glanced to see his brother had just returned home. He would need to eat. His playing had taken much of his stamina. He hoped Lucy was home, perhaps she would read to him again tonight. She was preoccupied last night, his brother's appetite outweighing his own. So he'd gone out to play with another.

"Whore!"

The word echoed down the street. A red-haired beauty fled from the front door, but his brother caught her arm in restraint. He didn't quicken, but watched as she turned and raised her knee into his brother's groin. There was a bellow of pain and his brother released her arm. She raised her knee again as he doubled over, striking him hard in the nose. His brother let out a grunt and she got away.

His gaze followed her to a small blue sedan where he saw Lucy sitting in the passenger's seat. His heart dropped in confusion when the door of the car closed. There was a popping echo and the shattering of glass. The car's tires squealed and sped down the street.

His brother stood in the middle of the street, panting venom.

"Where the hell have you been?" his brother demanded as he crossed the street.

"A date."

"Jesus fucking Christ, Jorge! What have I told you about dating?"

"I wore the gloves like you asked," he said as his brother growled in frustration. "Marco, where is Lucy going?"

"Shut up, Jorge!"

He followed his brother into the house and watched him stomp up the stairs. Jorge went to the kitchen for food. His brother yelled in frustration before Jorge heard a thump and a crash from the floor above.

He stood in front of the freezer and debated between taquitos and hot pockets. He wasn't sure which sounded better.

"I need you here now," his brother yelled into his phone as he walked into the kitchen.

I could eat the Philly cheese steak hot pockets, but we have the pepperoni pizza. I wonder if we even have sour cream . . .

"Fuck her . . . I'm talking about the necklace . . . Yes . . . fine. Whatever it takes."

Looks like just enough for seven and a quarter taquitos. Perfect.

Chapter Two

The rush of air and noise hit him like a drug, numbing his raging mind as he moved beyond the outer door of the hotel bar. Dressed in a dark leather jacket, t-shirt and jeans Detective Eric Stiles was looking forward to solace in the form of a strong drink. The place was packed and he made his way through the maze of people, reaching the edge of the bar.

"Jack Daniels on the rocks," he requested over the roar of the crowd as he grabbed a seat.

His hand wrapped around the smooth clear glass put in front of him. His mind flashed to his girlfriend of two years and his friend of over fifteen, half-naked on his couch. It stung. More than he cared to admit. He took the drink down in one gulp, and motioned to the bartender for another.

Three drinks later, Eric had almost erased the fact that his life was in shambles and realized that he was more disappointed than angry. He was disappointed that he'd let it get this far. He knew things were falling apart between them. He'd convinced himself that if he ignored the problem it would work itself out. They'd grown apart, as people do, wanting different things for the future and had come to an impasse. He focused on his work instead of dealing with it, and she slipped away into the arms of his friend. There wasn't anyone to blame. They'd given up and not bothered to tell the other.

The roar of noise emanating from the corner of the bar broke through his tirade of self-loathing. He was looking for a distraction. Eric grabbed his drink, pushing his way through the crowd to the apparent center of attention.

The two pool tables in the bar were surrounded by onlookers. He watched as a burly man called and took a shot. He made it and took another. Eric failed to see the attraction. The man missed his second shot and the crowd jeered in response. Not the distraction he was looking for, Eric was about to exit the scene when a flash of deep red caught his eye.

She moved around the table to survey her options. Her stance steady and strong, she carried herself with confidence, ignoring the appreciative and accusing eyes surrounding her. Deep red hair was a twisting of curls down her back, spilling over her forest green shirt. The fabric clung to her curves in all the right places, until its smooth lines were broken by her mid-hip loose fitting jeans. Leaning across the table, pool stick in hand, she pushed her hair behind her ear and chose her shot.

"Eleven off the sidewall into the nine and the fifteen, nine in the side, fifteen in the corner," she called in a cool even tone.

A burst of activity enveloped the room as money changed hands. The small area became quiet as they watched her take the shot. Eric heard the pop and watched as the eleven ball bounced back, off the sidewall, into the nine, and the nine into the fifteen. The nine ball dropped in the side, and everyone held their breath as the fifteen rolled along the rim, hesitated and dropped, just as the eleven fell into the opposite side.

The room erupted into cheers. He watched her focus remain on the game. She had a shot at the eight. Amid the chaos, Eric watched her once again survey her choices. The eight was in a precarious position. Eric worked out how he'd attempt the shot and wondered what her plan of attack would be.

"Two-hundred bucks says you miss the shot," her opponent called.

Eric watched for her response.

She looked over the table. She reached into her pocket, pulled out four hundreds and showed them to him. "Double or nothing."

The crowd erupted into whistles and catcalls as the man accepted her offer and the frenzied swarm watched her line up her shot. She called the side to her direct right. She lined up the shot and pulled back. The cue popped against the eight ball, spinning it as it shot down the table toward the opposite wall. It bounced and dropped clean into the pocket.

The entire mob erupted into cheers and Eric saw her smile for the first time as she met her challenger's stunned gaze. It wasn't a full smile, more of a smirk, as she nodded and dug her hand into her pocket. She lowered her head in humility, before her gaze lifted and landed on him. It was an instant, but it felt like hours as a rush of heat coursed through his body. He stood frozen within the shining hypnotic blue of her eyes.

The crowd began to disperse, and she looked away before disappearing within it, taking his breath with her. Eric moved forward, grabbing a pool cue. His mind buzzed with a wavy electricity that was intoxicating. He struggled to understand what just happened.

He played solo until a perky blonde by the name of Beth decided he needed company. Buried enough in his own mind not to care, Eric proceeded to play three games with the blonde. He finished their third game, she batted her eyes and he noticed a mane of cascading dark red hair sitting at the bar. He did his best to ignore the insistence in his gut, but found himself unable to deny his need to keep his gaze on her.

He finished his pool game and excused himself to the bar. Beth followed and Eric ordered a pair of beers for himself and his energetic friend. She took the seat next to him, placing herself between him and his mysterious preoccupation.

"Are you here on business or pleasure?" Beth asked him as the cascade of red behind her shifted and bright blue eyes appeared, meeting his gaze.

The spilling of curls framed her slim, oval face. They fell over her slender shoulders, leaving just a glimpse of the ivory of her curved neck.

"Layover," he replied to the blonde, but his eyes stayed within the enthralling swell of blue just behind her.

"What a coincidence, me, too! I'm headed to Chicago," the blonde said with a giggle. "So when does your flight leave?"

"Tomorrow morning," he replied, still focused behind her. His heart leapt a little as the blonde's captivating red-headed shadow smiled, her eyes sparkling.

"I guess it's good that I caught you when I did," the blonde continued, tracing the top of his hand with her finger.

"Yeah I guess it is," Eric replied, doing his best not to give away the charade.

"So do you have a girlfriend?" the blonde asked.

Eric watched her shadow turn from him before stepping away from the bar. "No, I uh . . ." he started to reply as he watched her go. His cell rang in his pocket. "Sorry, I have to take this."

"Hey, you saved my life," Eric said into the phone as he walked away from the bar. He followed in her footsteps as he searched for her. He stopped in the lobby of the hotel as his brother mumbled incoherent words in his ear. He agreed with him every couple of seconds as he scanned the area, seeing no sign of her. His stomach knotted in discomfort. He heard the whoosh of automatic doors open. Eric turned as she walked through them. "I'll call you later."

Her focus on the ground below, her hands hung from the pockets of her faded jeans as she re-entered the hotel. He waited for her to look up as he tried to think of what to say. When she did, her breathtaking smile once again made his heart skip.

"Hi," he managed to say as she stopped just in front of him.

"Hi," she replied, her eyes twinkling.

He was captivated by her and he forgot to articulate any of the dozens of thoughts running in his head. He could see a small blush rise in her cheeks.

"I'm going to go get some coffee across the street. Would you like to come?"

"Yeah, sure," he fumbled as she motioned toward the door.

The air was warm as she led him around the building. He could see the reflecting light of the coffee shop across the street as they turned the corner. "So you got stuck, too?"

"Yeah, but I'm on my way home," she replied, not looking at him as they walked. "Sounded like you're on your way . . . not home."

"Why do you say that?"

"You don't seem to be the east coast type," she replied with a small shrug. "No offense."

"None taken, I guess I didn't know there was a type associated with different coasts," he replied with a laugh.

"Oh yeah," she said. "There are certain characteristics that one picks up from the coast they live on. East coasters, for example. They're very suspicious people and aren't usually friendly off the bat, always guarded."

"So I'm friendly?" he asked as he opened the door to the coffeehouse for her.

"I didn't say that," she replied with a smile as they moved to the counter. They ordered coffees, paying separately before taking a seat at one of the small café tables. "You're . . . hesitant."

"Hesitant," Eric repeated, watching her relax into her seat, her chin resting on her hand. "I don't think I've ever heard anyone described like that."

"There's a first time for everything," she replied with a smirk as their coffee arrived.

"So what's home like?"

"I have a proposition."

"Shoot," he replied, intrigued.

"I propose that this conversation continue without specifics," she offered, her eyes challenging him. "Nothing personal, no names, no places, working generalities only."

"Okay, I'm game," he replied as he picked a random, non-personal question out of his head. "How much coffee do you drink a day?"

"Too much," she replied with a grin, fingering the edge of her cup. "Who's your favorite band?"

"Band or singer?"

"Band."

"STP, yours?"

"The Police. Singer?"

"Tough one, but I'd have to say George Strait."

"That's surprising."

"Yours?"

"Billy Joel."

"Nice choice," he complimented as she took another sip of her coffee. "Where did you learn to play pool like that?"

"Self-taught," she said, a smirk creeping onto the edges of her pale lips. "Pool table in the garage. First car?"

"Dodge Charger, yours?"

"Geo Metro."

"Drink of choice?"

"Corona."

"Shot?"

"Patron with a lime," she answered, her head tilting as she looked at him thoughtfully. "You like Jack, but your shot of choice, I would guess, is Quervo 500."

"A fellow tequila enthusiast, good call," he complimented before leaning into the table as he lowered his voice. "You don't want to go home."

"Neither do you," she countered, her eyes intelligent and steady. "Because of family or a relationship?"

"The latter," he replied, distracting himself with a drink of coffee as the images ran through his mind. "You?"

"The first," she said, flashing him a forced smile, her eyes revealing a hidden anxiety as she took a sip of her coffee. "Not sure which is worse."

"Family, always family," he replied, which made her laugh and lifted her out of the darkness that seemed to pull at her. "Other crap you can walk away from, but family? Family clings no matter how far you go. They will always be there."

"When you say it that way it doesn't seem too bad."

"Depends on the circumstances."

"So back to generalities, hypothetically."

"Yes, generalities . . ." Eric replied, conscious of her emanating warmth wrapping around him. "If you could choose any profession, what would it be?"

"Other than the one I already have?"

"Well that's up to you. I'm ignorant either way."

"Okay then," she replied, tapping her fingers on her cup. "A historian."

"Interesting."

"What?"

"Just not what I would've thought."

"And what would you've thought?"

"Honestly?"

"Yes."

"Lawyer."

"Lawyer?"

"Yeah."

"Wow," she replied with a chuckle as she stretched her back. "What made you say that?"

"I just . . . what little I do know about you, I think that you're good at making a strong argument."

"Okay . . ." she replied, tilting her head as she turned her cup in her hand. "What about you?"

"Teacher."

"You've thought about this."

"A little."

"If you could go anywhere in the world, where would you go?"

"All expenses paid?"

"Of course!"

"Egypt," he replied, watching for her reaction. "Where would you go?"

"Egypt, I want to see the pyramids."

"Interesting."

"A friend of mine went about a year ago and she said Hurghada is incredible."

"What about the Siwa Oasis?"

"There's no question," she replied. "Just to be able to observe the culture and the history. Can you imagine walking along the same path as Tut or Hatshepsut? It's just so amazing, the things they accomplished."

"Especially when you realize how much of their findings we still don't understand, even with all the cutting edge technology."

"I'm an Egypt freak," she admitted with a small blush.

"Anytime anything about the pyramids or Egypt is on television, I set it to record."

"I must have at least two dozen shows sitting on my DVR at home," he added, a heat rising in his neck as his eyes caught hers again. "Did you see that one on the door they found beneath the Sphinx?"

"The Library," she replied, her eyes widening in intrigue. "The one where they were about to go in and the Egyptian government shut them down?"

They became engulfed in a mutual banter about all things related to the pyramids and Egypt. The conversation drifted off to other general topics, including a heated debate about the Lakers' offensive triangle and the musings of Anderson Cooper.

Eric wasn't sure how much time had passed when they headed back to the hotel, still laughing and talking. He walked into the lobby and the thought of saying goodbye to her twisted an unfamiliar knot in his stomach.

"I should probably get to bed," she said as she turned to him, her hands in her pockets. "My flight leaves pretty early."

"Yeah, me, too," he replied with an uncomfortable nod. "Thanks for the company. It was fun."

"It was," she replied as her eyes locked with his. She leaned forward, placing a soft kiss on his cheek. "Night."

"Night," he replied, his breath catching in his throat as he watched her turn the corner and disappear.

He wanted to go after her, he wanted to know her name, and yet his feet remained cemented to the floor. He dug into his pocket, found his room key and moved to the elevator. He pushed the button for his floor, as he rationalized letting her walk away. They would never see each other again. Which was the whole reason, he assumed, that she wanted to keep it all in generalities.

She was just a stranger he'd met in a bar, a captivating, intelligent, funny, beautiful stranger, but a random stranger nonetheless. He didn't need to complicate his life more than it already was. Walking away was the right thing to do.

Chapter Three

Eric stepped onto his floor and looked at his key for the room number. He turned the corner, seeing her mane of curls tossed over her shoulder. She dug in her pocket while balancing two bottles of water in one hand. After a moment, she looked up, meeting his eyes and all sense of reason disintegrated as his body ignited.

"Old hangover trick," she explained with a smile. He moved toward her, needing to shorten the unbearable gap. All of his energy fell into the ocean of her eyes as he invaded her space. Her voice faded as his hand rested on her hip. "Two Tylenol and a bottle . . ."

His fingertips grazed over the delicate twists framing her face. Her eyes fluttered closed and a powerful need overwhelmed him. His hand wrapped around her waist to land on the small of her back. He pulled her against him, feeling the gentle rise of her chest as she took a slow breath. He focused on her eyes as they opened, and he lowered his mouth to brush a hesitant kiss over her breathtaking lips.

The touch was soft and lingering. She moved her lips against his in a tender caress that made his heart flutter. Unable to ignore the softness of her lips, he savored every touch. His fingertips swept her cheek as he kissed her long and slow. The water in her hands dropped to the floor with a soft thud. She wrapped her arms around his shoulders and his hand tangled itself within the curled tendrils of her beautiful hair.

The delicate scent of her body filled him, stirred the rolling heat within his stomach and a groan sat at the bottom of his throat. He ached for her skin as his hands shifted beneath her shirt. His fingers danced over the silk of her lower back. Her soft body crashed against him. Her grazing hands inched down his back, across his abdomen and up to his chest, sending spikes of electricity into his groin.

Their once hesitant, tender embrace became deep, insistent and brimmed with mutual passion. One hand in her hair, the other encircling her waist and he walked her back, trapping her against the wall. His hunger for her seemed unquenchable as he devoured her lips and explored the recesses of her mouth with his tongue.

His heated body pressed against hers as their lips parted, gasping for air. He traced his tongue down the line of her neck. He stopped, suckling on her collarbone. His fingers lingered on the area of satin between the dip of her waist and the curve of her hip. They played for a moment before moving upward, across her ribs. She attacked his ear with a purr. He lifted his eyes, the reflection of his own breathless passion shone within her depths of blue.

"Where's your room?" she managed to ask as he tugged at her lips in distraction.

"I have no idea," he said with a grin. She cocked her head to the side before her hands dove into his pockets. Searching for his key, her fingers brushed against his stiffening cock.

Unable to turn away from her dazzling eyes, a smile edged his mouth as she teased him. When she finished, she drew him against her by the pocket of his jeans.

"I think I found it," she said as her breath teased his lips.

She triumphantly lifted the key between them.

Room three forty-eight.

Content just to have her in his arms, he realized he didn't care about the room or the world around them. Overwhelmed by the new sensation of serenity, his thumb traced the line of her cheek. He leaned down, once again coaxing her lips against his. Her arms slid around his neck as she brought him closer. He fell into the candy of her mouth.

Voices descended the hall and she whimpered in irritation at the interruption. He groaned with the broken embrace as he took her hand to search for his room. She laughed at his obvious desperation.

An unnerving ache replaced the serenity in the absence of her warmth. As soon as he found the room, he swept her back into his arms and pressed her against the door. He reclaimed her lips as his own, in case she'd forgotten. His hands slid around her hips before he lifted her, and she wrapped her legs around his waist.

He carried her into the room. His attention still focused on her lips as the door closed somewhere off in the distance. Her legs locked around his waist as she pushed his leather jacket off his shoulders and he shrugged it away. The edge of the bed bumped against his leg. He lifted his knee as he turned and leaned forward, laying her down beneath him.

Their lips parted as he eased against her, their bodies meeting through the barrier of cloth. His encased cock rubbed against her jean-clothed pussy, tingles of arousal spiking between them. His fingers traced the edge of her hair. He gazed into her eyes, making sure they both knew where this was going. She seemed to sense his hesitation and answered it with a sunlit smile and a grind of her hips that erased any of his doubts.

He'd never wanted someone so much in his entire life . . .

His body recognized the pulsing need, but it had a slow steady rhythm that he wanted to last. He covered and caressed her lips. Despite their body's inflamed demands, the urgency turned into tenderness and longing.

He rolled her on top of him. His hands reveled in the heat of her body as the softness beneath his fingers sent throbs of need through him. He tore at her neck as her hands scorched the skin beneath his shirt. Her nails were circling and playing against his sensitive nerves as her lips attached to his ear.

She straddled him, breaking the embrace as she lifted and pulled her shirt over her head. Her hair fell around him as she met his lips. He couldn't help but push his fingers into the beautiful cascade of fire. She smiled, teasing his lips.

She attacked his chest with her tongue, as she pushed up his shirt. He stifled a groan of delight while he caressed the smooth planes of her back. She nipped at his chest and latched onto a nipple, her teasing setting him aflame. He gripped her hips and rolled her back beneath him. His hips nestled against hers, his aching cock pushed against her pussy. She pulled him tighter with her legs as she shifted her hips, her pelvis rubbing against his length.

She pulled his shirt up and off as her fingers skimmed over his chest and arms. Chills rushed through him as her exploration mixed with the heat emanating from her pelvic teasing. Her discoveries erupted in his chest as soft sighs. He opened his eyes to the sight of her perfect mouth lifting to kiss his chest as her tongue rolled across him like oil on a hot pan. The sensuality of it shot indescribable pressure into his body and he fought his own animal instincts to not claim her body right then.

He tugged on her earlobe with his teeth. His bare skin met hers and her tongue taunted the nerves behind his ear and down his neck, as his skin tingled.

Unrelenting, her feather touch trailed his back, circled his waist and stopped at the button of his jeans. Her hand grasped his cock through his pants and stroked the bulge. Spasms of unparalleled hunger pushed through the core of his body.

His blood turned liquid fire. Her caress ignited the smoldering flames of his arousal and his entire body groaned in response. His hands edged her ribs. He nipped at her neck and shoulders. She arched her back, allowing him to slip beneath and unclasp her bra.

He used his teeth to pull it down her shoulders. He tossed it away before laying claim to a succulent nipple. He suckled before encircling it and flicking it with his tongue. This incited gasps from her flawless lips and the pad of his thumb took over as he relished in the second pink nipple. He teased and suckled, delighting in the whimpers that escaped her chest as he brought the second bud to a taut peak of arousal.

His hands covered her breasts as he kissed his way up to her perfect lips. Her hard peaks rolled against the palms of his hands. He nuzzled her neck, twisting his tongue while devouring the honey beneath his lips. Her fingertips lined his abs, pushing waves of heat through him. He continued to fondle her nipples into a frenzy before moving down and circling her tight stomach with his fingertips.

Her muscles tensed in apprehension beneath his fingers as he continued to tease. He heard her rushing breath and felt her nails curling against his neck just before he dipped beneath the cusp of her jeans.

His body pulsed at her reaction and he wanted her pleasure to edge and overflow. He took his time to explore her warmth as his mouth fed on her neck. He found her shaved pussy moist with anticipation as he pushed his middle finger against her lace panties, dipping into the opening of her vagina. Her hips rose in response and he slipped his fingers beneath the lace. Separating his fingers into a V he lined the inside of her labia, consciously avoiding her clit. His fingers reunited at the bottom of her vagina where they joined.

He rested the heel of his hand on the top of her pelvis as he cupped her moist cunt. The movement put the slightest of controlled pressure against her clit. He savored the sound of her sharp intake of breath against his ear before her hips lifted, pressing into his hand. His whole hand began to massage her and Eric lifted his eyes to her beautiful face.

His own passion flared as he watched her body become tight and focused, writhing beneath his massaging hand. He wanted to push her further. He parted her mouth with his tongue as he shifted and slipped the joined fingers into her dripping cunt. Her back arched against his penetrating digits. His kiss captured a wanting moan and his own desire roared as he began to slowly finger fuck her tight pussy, his thumb brushing her clit. Her body bent beneath his hand as her mouth revealed the depths of her desire. He played with her, building the pressure within.

She broke their embrace with a whimper and a twist beneath his hand. His ministrations ceased as she rolled against him. Her lips became insistent and her hands skimmed over him with a purpose. She taunted him with the tips of her nails as she took her time unbuttoning his pants. She slid beneath his jeans and her warm hand wrapped around his pulsing cock.

His hands in her hair, he teased her mouth with his tongue. She began pulling, squeezing and massaging.

God, she knows what she's doing . . .

He moved against her tantalizing grip as the tip of her finger swirled precum around the head of his cock. Eric cursed aloud as his arousal heightened into a frantic state. He was unable to suppress the desperate groan that escaped his chest as she continued turning him to steel. He grasped her hips and trapped her beneath him as he ravaged her mouth.

His body howled in desire. He wanted to be inside her, he wanted to feel her cunt engulf him. He gasped for air as he pulled off the bed to discard his jeans. He watched her crawl toward the edge of the bed, and his mind transfixed on the curve of her body. It rose to meet him as her pink nipples peaked beneath her hair. Her slim waist led down to her rounded hips and he forgot what he was about to do. Her hands hooked into the loops of his jeans and pulled him forward.

He drowned in the sight of her. He couldn't believe how intoxicating she was and how his body reacted to her every breath. Her hands spread over his abdomen and his body tingled as she began enticing his senses with her mouth. His eyes closed in elation.

She pressed soft, slow kisses across his chest and shoulders as her hands roamed. His nerves melted with her journey, firing tiny bursts of electricity beneath her mouth. She tugged at his zipper and his fingers threaded themselves in her hair. Her lips continued down and he lost his breath. Her hand wrapped around him, releasing his cock from the binding of his pants. He felt her moist tongue trail from his base to the tip.

He looked to see her eyes smoldering as she watched him. Her soft mouth encircled the head of his cock, sending blind molten pleasure through his body. His breath turned heavy, but his eyes remained steady with hers, while he twirled her hair between his fingers.

She slid her mouth down his shaft as her tongue teased. She took him in, completely swallowing him within her tight hot mouth and a gasp of pleasure escaped his lips. She held still for a moment and then began stroking him with her tongue as her head moved back and forth.

He didn't know if he could contain the fire she created within her amazing mouth. Her ministrations pushed the limits of his restraint and he lost his mind. He dug his hands into her hair with a groan as he swelled within her mouth. He pulled her up and met her torturous gaze as she licked her lips like a satisfied cat. She kept her hand around him as he lifted her chin and seized her mouth.

He gathered her up and off the bed. His mouth dominated her as he pinned her against the wall. Edging the fullness of her lips with his tongue, he shifted, breathing kisses down her cheek before suckling the pulse of her neck.

She released soft coos as her fingers skimmed across his shoulders. His hands trailed over her body before they rubbed against her hardened nipples. He heard her gasp and powerful shots of lightning bolted through him as his need for her intensified.

His hands slid against the curve of her waist and over the swell of her hips. His tongue made a trail down her body until he reached her navel. He made quick work of removing what remained of her clothing. His hands feathered up the sides of her legs.

He kissed the softness just inside her right knee as he lifted it over his shoulder. He breathed her scent in before kissing the rosy lips of her pussy. He unrolled his tongue, tasting the sweetness of her moisture. He licked up and around her labia, teasing the area surrounding her erect clit.

Her hands burrowed into his hair as her entire body tensed and shivered beneath the exploring of his mouth. He used his tongue to continue to tease her before he thrust it into her awaiting cunt. He pushed inside of her, devouring the delicious moisture of her pussy. Her hips twisted in need and he shifted, his mouth and tongue focusing on her screaming clit. Sucking it between his lips, he flicked it with the tip of his tongue. He locked onto it with his entire mouth, hearing her cries of aroused frustration as he brought her just to the edge of bliss.

Her breath came in gasps and whimpers. He replaced his mouth with the light touch of his hand as he kissed his way back up her body. Eric nuzzled her neck. He could feel her shuddering, knowing that she was close as he kept her body writhing with the feather brush of his middle finger.

"Let go," he whispered into her ear as his hand stroked her fire.

The effect of his teasing mouth was felt in the pulsing

shivers riveting her body. He knew what he was asking. His breath became rough within his chest as the anticipation of it increased the pressure inside his groin. To see her let go within his arms as he pleasured her would be incredible. He pressed her lips to his. Caressing her mouth more than kissing it as he wrapped his arm around her back, cushioning her against the wall.

"Trust me."

Her leg lifted and bent against his thigh as her foot flattened on the wall behind her. His kisses remained soft and tender as he worshiped her. She let out a shuddered breath against his lips. Her nails gripped at his neck as her mouth communicated her need. His own body came alive, his cock twitching in need against her waiting hand. His thumb pressed against her clit as he slipped two fingers into her dripping cunt and began their slide in and out. Heated breaths and sweet moans escaped from her chest.

His lips continued to caress her mouth as her body shivered and tightened in torrents beneath his hand. He maintained his steady but gentle manipulation of her body. Her hips ground in union with his hand as she cupped her own breast. His own desire for her threatened his control.

He focused on the beauty of her angelic face. Her eyes half-closed as she gasped for air, she was exquisite. Her forehead rested against his cheek as her body swayed in desire, and his inflamed nerves raged as her hand gripped and pulled the length of his cock.

He lined her neck with his tongue before sweeping back with a heated breath. He was desperate to control his increasing hunger as her hand twisted and pulled. Her cheeks reddened and her lips parted as her lashes fluttered over her magnificent eyes in focused rapture. The hunger in his groin intensified into a harsh pulsing ache.

He wanted to quench the building heat within her. He

curled his hand's movement and hit the softness of her g-spot. She gasped in ecstasy. He focused on it, the head of his fingers thrusting against it repeatedly. He started slow and then picked up speed, circling her clit in time with his thrusts. Her back arched off the wall and she met his movement as her head fell back in a gasp of building pleasure.

A rush of unimaginable lust filled him as he witnessed her ascending pleasure. He wanted so badly to replace his hand with his cock it physically hurt. His mouth pushed against the hollow of her neck and trailed down before he leaned down and grazed at a nipple with the flat of his tongue.

He rubbed the succulent peak with his tongue and it hardened even more. Her nails dug into his shoulder as her entire form tensed.

He pinched her nipple as he nuzzled her ear, "Cum for me, baby."

"Oh God," she gasped. Her delicate body shuddered against him as the waves of her climax began to wash over her body. She let out a cry of pure bliss, the caress of her pulsing explosion making him frantic in hungry desire, as his own restraint began to fail.

He pulled his dripping hand away, lifting it to his mouth. He licked his hand clean, savoring the taste of her, before suckling the nape of her neck. His hand rested against the base of her spine as she lifted herself to his lips. Her sweet breath came in small pants as her body continued to quiver.

"You're so beautiful," he said, capturing her dreamy eyes. He repossessed her mouth as his arms cradled her against him. His kisses remained gentle and tender as he heard her whimper.

She pushed at his pants in urgent need. She groaned in frustration and he discarded them. Eric kept his arms around her as if protecting her from the surrounding darkness.

Astounded by her splendor, his entire body hardened and ached in smoldering passion as he laid her on the bed. He hovered over her, breathless as he slipped on a condom. Her enchanting eyes lifted to him with a coaxing caress as his rigid cock slipped into the incredible warmth of her pussy.

A deep groan pushed from the depths of his chest. His senses flared uncontrolled as his body absorbed the marvelous heat that enveloped him. She arched against him. The shift pulled him deeper and he hit bottom as a flash of breathless fever burst through him. Her welcoming pussy tightened around him. A wave of ravenous heat pulsed through his body, and his hunger for her peaked beyond his control.

He leaned forward, kissing her, as they relented to a mutual ache. He began his movement. Pulling his cock out of her cunt and then plunging back in. He relished every stroke of her delicious body's caress. Her hips rose and fell in time with his, as they settled into a luscious harmony. It was silk, smooth and rhythmic, each thrust within her more effectual and deeper than the last.

Earthy whimpers and billowing soft moans of euphoria poured out of her. They fanned the blaze breathing within her body. Sheathed within the incredible warmth of her pussy it pulsed around him, milking the cum out of him.

Their fueled need for each other heightened with each joined breath, each heated touch, each moan of delight, and she arched against his chest as his thrusts became harder and faster. He reached between them, pressing her clit beneath his thumb. She drowned him and cried out in release. Her pleasure shattered against him. The pulse of her ecstasy pushed him further as his thrusts tightened and he plunged over the edge of his own precipice. His body pulled her in and then exploded into a brilliant white light of weightlessness.

Her softness shivered beneath him, sending residual sparks of electricity bursting through his body. He caught his breath as he tugged and played with her lips. He relaxed within her embrace, his cock still buried deep within her body. His mouth lingered and deepened as he kissed her, never wanting to stop.

The soothing feel of her nails brushed through his hair. Her hand on his shoulder, he shifted, gazing down into her beguiling eyes. Her soft hands framed his face. She looked up at him with tender expressive eyes and for the first time in his life, his heart calmed. Time ceased in the cushion of warmth as a serenity he never dared to imagine encompassed him.

She shifted, and gathering her into his arms, he pulled her with him as he rolled onto his side. She curled into him and the unexpected need to continue to have her against him began to ease. He tugged the blankets of the bed up and around them before his arm wrapped around her.

He released a deep breath as her cheek rested on his shoulder. He relaxed into the pull of exhaustion, with a sense of complete contentment. He kissed the top of her head as he brushed his fingers through her hair. She seemed to melt into him as his eyes closed, and they drifted off into a peaceful slumber.

The phone blared in his ear and he shifted, opening his eyes as he reached for it.

"Hello," Eric said, demanding his brain to work.

"This is your 6 AM wake up call. Good Morning, Mr. Stiles," he heard as he let out a long sigh, pushing his hands over his scalp.

"Thanks," he said before hanging up the phone and his mind caught up to the events of last night. He remembered her beautiful smile. He searched the bed for her, and found a note.

I'll never forget . . .

She was gone.

CHAPTER FOUR

Rebecca Gailen walked into the bullpen of the professional staffing firm where she worked and headed to her private office. Her cell phone rang. She pulled it from the pocket of her purse, looked at the number and answered.

"Hey, sweetie," she said feeling her stomach roll as she heard her younger sister's voice.

"Beccs, you need to get me out of here."

"Lucy, you're going to be fine, you just need to hang in there," Rebecca replied as her heart broke at the sound of her sister's tortured pleas.

"I can't . . . I can't take it, Beccs. They're hurting me."

"You need to let them help you."

"I'll be good, I promise, Beccs. I just want to come home."

"Sweetheart, you need to get better first."

"I can't believe you did this! Why did you do this to me," Lucy started, her voice rising in betrayal and anger. "Get me out of here, Beccs, or I swear to God . . ."

"Lucy, stop. You need to calm down. I didn't do this to you."

"Yes you did! You hate me, you always have!"

"Lucy, you know I love you."

"No you don't! You want me to just disappear!"

"No I don't . . ."

"*I hate you*! Do you hear me? I hate you! You aren't my sister! You're *dead*, Beccs! *I hate you*!"

"Lucy," Rebecca tried to interrupt in an attempt to keep the upheaval of emotion from spilling beyond her control.

She continued to scream at her, but Rebecca heard someone talking to Lucy, telling her to calm down. Lucy continued to scream and the sound became more distant.

"Rebecca," she heard a familiar male voice. "She's okay."

Dr. Schaffer had been a friend of their mother's. So when Rebecca found Lucy drugged and out of control in Seattle, he was the first person she called. He ran a drug treatment hospital just outside Vegas. She was close enough that Rebecca could be there if she needed her, but still far enough away that she wasn't hovering.

"I know," she replied, her hand rising to her forehead. It had been a few weeks and it was going to take time.

"She's making progress. This has been her first bad day in a while."

"I want to come see her."

"That's not the best idea right now. Call me at the end of the week and we'll talk about it," he replied and she took a deep breath. "She's going to be okay, Rebecca. You just need to hang in there."

"Okay," Rebecca replied. "Please call me if you need anything."

"Of course. We'll talk to you soon," he replied as she hung up the phone and restarted her path across the office.

She pushed the guilt away and lowered her shoulders as she opened the door.

"You've got to be freaking kidding me," she said in irritation as she stepped in the office and saw an oversized Teddy Bear sitting in her chair, waiting. She placed her computer bag aside her desk. She turned on her heel and walked out of the office to her assistant's desk. "A teddy bear?"

"I thought he was cute," Mindy, her partner in crime, replied with a small smile.

"Fine," Rebecca replied as she walked back into the office, pushing her deep red curls off her shoulder in frustration.

She grabbed the bear off the chair. It was heavier than she expected, and she carried it out of the office and back to Mindy's desk.

"Then you take it home. Think of it as an early birthday present."

"Don't you think you're overreacting just a tad?" Mindy asked as she followed her back into the office. Mindy had been her friend for almost six years. They'd started with the company together and while Mindy's title was assistant, it was self-imposed. She had a loathing for any type of work-related responsibility, so she *assisted* Rebecca with hers.

"No. The whole thing is annoying and distracting."

"And romantic," Mindy offered, swinging her long brown ponytail off her shoulder as she arranged files on Rebecca's desk.

"So not romantic, Min," Rebecca objected as she pulled out her laptop and booted it up. "I have no idea who's sending all of this stuff to me. It's not romantic, it's disturbing!"

"Okay, I admit it," Mindy replied with a sigh, as she took a seat across from Rebecca's desk, her petite frame swallowed by the oversized chair. "I wasn't buying the romantic thing either. I was just trying to put a positive spin on it."

"There is no positive spin," Rebecca stated as she began reading her emails. "So what's going on today, besides back-to-back conference calls starting at one?"

"Nothing but the quarterly review," Mindy said and Rebecca looked to her in pain. "I'll get coffee."

"Good idea," Rebecca agreed as she took a deep breath and turned her attention back to her e-mail.

The day went on in a blur of emails, reports and questions. A few hours later, Rebecca heard Mindy say she was heading off to get food when her cell rang.

"This is Rebecca."

"Hey, do you want coffee?"

"I would love some."

"Okay, I'll be up in a few minutes," Charlie said before hanging up.

Rebecca laid the phone back on her desk, staring down at it and wondering if this was a good idea. She adored Charlie, and it had all started just as any solid relationship should. They began as friends, had fun together, and now he was ready to move it to the next level.

They'd gone on two official dates so far, and she'd had no complaints. How could she? Charlie was a handsome, gentle, sweet guy. On top of that, he had a stable income, his own place, and didn't do drugs. What more could a girl want?

The problem was, she knew what she wanted. She also knew she'd never have it.

Get over it, Rebecca! You're being ridiculous!

A knock at the door pulled her from her mind. She turned, seeing the familiar tall muscular man with tousled blond hair and amused hazel eyes standing in her doorway.

"Hey, Beccs," Charlie greeted as he walked into the office.

"That was fast."

"I aim to please."

"You're a god," she said with a nod as she took a sip and moved to the couch in the center of her office. "So what are you doing downtown, did something happen with the bar?"

It was an unwritten local rule that you only ventured downtown when absolutely necessary. As a resident of Sin City, you learn that downtown Vegas is a trial size New York, except with a blistering desert sun. So the locals avoided it at all costs.

Charlie's stable income came from a local bar he owned on the outskirts of town called the Rustic. It was where they'd first met. She'd come to hustle some pool and he took notice of her skills.

"I had to pick up my training paperwork and thought I

would come by and say hi."

"Liar, you're checking up on me."

"Maybe, but I did have to stop by the unit office."

Along with being a walking fantasy, Charlie was a patriot and served in the reserves once a month.

"You don't have to," she objected as he took a seat next to her on the couch. "I'm fine."

"I know, I just worry about you," he admitted as he leaned forward, kissing her.

"I do appreciate it, even if there's nothing to worry about."

He'd come to see if she'd received any more presents from her secret admirer. She had, but she was going to be damned if she told him about them. Rebecca had been receiving flowers and gifts from an unknown source for two weeks now.

Charlie happened upon the affair when she borrowed his truck. A·plethora of flowers had arrived from her admirer the previous week. She decided instead of letting them go to waste, she would take them to the local nursing home. She didn't do a very good job of erasing the evidence and was forced to explain.

"Beccs, you need to file a report with the police."

"I'm not having this argument with you again," she replied as she rose from the couch, moving away from him.

"Why are you being so stubborn about this?"

"Why are you making this a bigger deal than it needs to be?"

"Because it is a big deal."

"It's harmless," she replied with a smirk. "It's annoying, but harmless."

"And what if it gets dangerous?"

"It won't," she objected, and he met her eyes with a stern stare, not amused by her light attitude toward the situation.

"Fine, if it gets out of control, I'll file a report, okay?"

"Okay," he replied as he rose and pulled her into a hug. "I need to get back to work."

"So do I," she said as she hugged him back, kissing him on the cheek.

"Are we still on for dinner tonight?"

"Definitely," she replied with a smile. "I'll meet you at seven?"

"Seven it is," he replied with a smile as he stepped back to give her a kiss on the cheek before leaving. "I'll see you then."

Chapter Five

He twisted the cap off an unopened bottle of Vault as he took a seat at his desk. He pushed his hand through his hair and opened the file that sat in front of him. The Major Crime Unit of the Las Vegas Police Department was a buzz of activity. The entire department was on alert with their latest set of cases. Detective Eric Stiles was finishing his eighteenth hour running and ready for some much needed rest.

"Where are we?" his partner Adam asked as he approached, looking a little more awake than he had a few hours ago.

"Knee deep in shit."

"What else is new?" Adam replied as he took a seat at the desk across from Eric's. They worked for the next hour when Adam broke the silence. "You almost finished with that box?"

Eric and Adam had been partners for over eight years. Next to his brother, Charlie, he was one of Eric's closest friends. He'd been the best man at Adam's wedding and was godfather to his two-year-old daughter, Selena. They were family.

"Yeah, I would start on the next one, X45778," Eric replied as he focused on the crime scene photos attached to the file.

"Matheson, Stiles, you're up," they heard their captain shout from his office and they both grabbed their stuff and headed out.

As they pulled up to the building, Eric saw the perimeter

of police tape and a handful of officers taking statements. They walked beneath the tape and entered the scene, following the trail of officers to a *private room.*

"What've we got?" Adam asked as they took in the scene.

"Female, twenty-three years old," the responding officer described as Eric took in the spatter of blood that pinwheeled the room.

"Does she work here?"

"Yeah, she started a couple of months ago," the officer replied, looking at his notes. "She goes by the name Amber-Lynn but her real name is Veronica Naltin."

"Did anyone see anything?" Eric asked as he took a good look at the victim.

"No one saw or heard anything until one of the other girls found the body."

"Did we find the murder weapon?" Adam asked with as he glanced at Eric.

"Not inside, but we have guys checking the dumpsters and surrounding storm drains," the officer replied with a nod.

"Okay, thanks," Adam replied as Eric rose to his feet. "Where do you want to start?

"Let's start with the manager."

Five hours later, Eric sat at his desk, facing a now flat bottle of Vault.

His vision was beginning to blur and he couldn't focus. "I need to get some sleep."

"I'm surprised you're still sitting there," Adam replied with a shake of his head.

Eric rose from his desk and headed to the cage. The area was designed for officers to get much needed rest without having to leave the station. The soundproof whitewashed room became their second home when big cases hit. Eric opened the door to find that he wasn't the only one in need of rest. He saw three of his colleagues snoozing on various bunk beds throughout the room. Eric found a bed that looked comfortable, loosened his tie and lay down.

He closed his eyes. His mind floated and swam through the grayness behind them. He pushed away images and notes of the current investigation. He ignored the fact that he hadn't seen anyone or done anything outside the office in weeks. His body sank deeper into the cushion of the bed and began to relax.

An incessant vibration against his leg pulled him from the place of warmth. He tried to ignore it, but then lifted it out of his pocket and saw his brother's name.

"Charlie, what's up?" he greeted as he rose from the bed and ventured toward the door.

"I need your help."

"Why, what's wrong?" Eric said in immediate hesitation as he stepped into the hallway.

"It's this woman I'm dating—"

"Jesus. Charlie you scared the crap out of me . . ."

"Sorry."

"Look, I don't have time to talk right now," Eric said as he fought to keep his eyes open. "I need to—"

"One question."

"Fine, go."

"What do I do if I think someone is being stalked?"

"What the—"

"You said you didn't have time to talk."

"Fine, you need to come down and file a report," Eric replied in confusion. "The DSU will look into it and issue a restraining order against the suspect."

"What if I don't know who is doing it?"

"What do you mean?"

"What if the stalking is anonymous?"

"Okay, maybe you should . . ." Eric started and then saw Adam looking up at him from the bottom of the stairs. Eric nodded to him and started down the stairs toward him. "Charlie, I'm going to need to call you back. Look, just come down or have whoever come down and file a report. I gotta go."

It was early and quiet. She loved coming into the office before the crack of dawn. She could concentrate and get work done without interruption. Rebecca went through her emails one by one and after about an hour, rose to get some coffee. She walked into the staff kitchen and pulled out the cream.

Her mind wandered and landed in the comfort of his deep eyes. She remembered the warmth of his arms and wished she was with him now. Maybe if she was, she'd be able to relax. Perhaps get some sleep and shake off the dread that seemed to have encapsulated her.

Keep dreaming . . . you'll never see him again . . .

While she told Mindy and Charlie that the gifts and attention didn't bother her, it did. She refused to give into the almost screaming demand for a reaction from her. That's what he wanted. He wanted to get to her, good or bad. He was looking for some kind of validation. She could only hope that if she stayed strong long enough that he would wake up and realize what he was doing was wrong.

She shook herself out of her head and looked down to see that she'd filled her cup. Her head buzzed as she walked back into her office and tried to refocus on her emails. His smile kept popping into her mind and she struggled to shut it out. She had Charlie. He is so wonderful and she . . . adored him.

God what the hell is wrong with me?

She growled in frustration.

"Good morn . . ." the unexpected voice sent a spike of fear through her and she jumped out of her chair.

"Whoa, Beccs, it's just me," Mindy said as she looked at her in alarm. "Are you okay?"

"Sorry, I just . . ." she started, her heart pounding in her chest. She tried to breathe and found it difficult. "I just . . . had too much coffee this morning."

"Okay note to self, Beccs gets decaf for the rest of the day."

"Yeah, really," Rebecca added with a laugh. "What are you doing here so early?"

"What are you talking about? I'm half an hour late."

Rebecca looked out her door and saw that the once empty office was now bustling with activity and she'd somehow blocked it out.

"Are you sure you're okay, sweetie?"

"Yeah, I'm fine," Rebecca replied with another laugh. "So what's on the agenda today?"

"Three conference calls and two meetings," Mindy replied as she handed her a folder. "Light day."

"Let's hope so," Rebecca replied as she took the folder with a smile. "We need to look at the wage balances before the eleven."

"I'll pull the report and be right back."

"Thanks, Mindy."

Rebecca watched as she walked out of the room. She took a deep breath and looked back to her email, determined to focus when her phone rang.

"This is Rebecca," she said hearing one of the other staffing consultants on the other end. She got deep into the conversation and then saw her IM flashing a new message.

Hi, Beccs.

She looked at it, not recognizing the screen name, bldlvr928.

Hi. Who is this?

When she got no answer, she closed the window and re-focused on her conversation. A few moments went by and she saw she had a response. Distracted, she opened it. She remained focused on what her caller was saying as she sat back in her chair.

Having a good morning so far? You got here early this morning. You could use a break. Don't you think?

Rebecca read the dialog in curiosity when the lights flashed and the fire alarm sounded throughout the building. Rebecca said goodbye to the woman on the phone and looked back to her computer screen in confusion.

See you soon, Beccs.

"Rebecca, come on," Mindy called to her and she followed her out of the building.

Eric got out of the car and walked with Adam to the yellow-taped area. They stepped beyond the barrier. It was quiet, no hoards of onlookers or witnesses to interview. Just the hotel manager who might be able to give them a description of the suspect, if he rented the room.

The girl's deep red hair was fanned across the blood-soaked bed. Her blue eyes were staring at them and a chill went up his spine. Her body was covered in lacerations, some extensive and others a few inches long. Two deep slices across each of her upper arms were the source of the pooling blood and he guessed the cause of death.

They went through the scene, talked to the witnesses. Time of death was a little after midnight. The hotel manager described the woman with no problem, but never saw her companion, male or female. He reported nothing out of the ordinary until the maid staff found the body.

Eric waited just outside the room as Adam finished up. His mind was distracted and he knew why. The victim brought her into his mind. He saw her eyes, and he struggled to push the image of her away. He didn't want to think of her now. Not here.

Eric took a deep breath and reminded himself that he was tired and hungry. He always became a little unhinged when those two needs were lacking. He'd bounce back and return to reality once he had some food in him.

"Stiles, what's up?"

"Ah . . . nothing," Eric replied as he shook his head and they started toward the car.

"You sure?"

"Yeah, just need some food."

When they returned to the office, a stack of surveillance discs were left sitting on their desks. And two desks away was a box of cold pizza. Five hours later, Eric and Adam were still looking through the footage from the previous crime scene. They'd seen a blur of faces and nothing out of the ordinary.

Eric switched discs when Adam's phone rang. He could tell by the smile on his partner's face that his wife, Olivia, was on the other end. He'd met her through a mutual friend, they were an automatic fit and things just progressed from there.

If it could be that easy . . .

He, on the other hand, hadn't ever been lucky in the romance department. He had no tolerance for the games or the wooing. He just wanted what he wanted, when he wanted it. Choice women, his ex included, called it chauvinistic and pig headed, but to him, it was honest. He didn't have time for anything complicated or full of drama. He needed to find someone who was there when he needed them and out of the way when he didn't. No heartstrings, roses or poems . . . just real and honest.

Eric leaned back in his chair and thought of Dallas. He wondered what she was like, in reality. In his mind, she was the perfect woman, but here in the real world, who knew?

His phone rang, he saw it was Charlie.

"Charlie."

"Do you have time to talk?"

"Yeah what's up?"

"A friend of mine is in some trouble."

"Is this concerning the stalker that you asked about?"

"Yeah."

"Tell me what's been going on."

"It started with cards and gifts at the office. Last week, she got dozens of bouquets sent to her house and the office."

"And she says she has no idea who they're from?"

"Right and it's escalating . . ."

"Charlie . . ."

"I don't think she's telling me everything either. I know there's more going on . . ."

"You need to get her to come in and file a report," Eric explained with a sigh. "There's nothing we can do until she comes down and talks to the Domestic Violence Unit."

"Okay, I will try and convince her."

"If anything else happens, you need to call it into the police, Charlie. This is serious and you need to do everything you can to get her down here to talk to someone before it gets too far out of control."

"Okay. I will," Charlie replied with a heavy sigh. "Where the hell have you been, man, I haven't seen you in weeks."

"Yeah, I've been a little busy."

"Have you heard from Robyn?"

Eric winced a little at the mention of his ex. "She's left a couple of messages, but I haven't called her back."

"How was the wedding?"

"Interesting."

"Is that so? Care to share the details?"

"That is definitely a story for another time," Eric replied with a laugh as Adam waved to get his attention. "Hey, I

have to go."
    "Okay, thanks for your help."
    "Sure."
    "Oh and call Dad, or he's going to show up there."
    "Thanks for the warning."
    "That's what brothers are for. Later."

CHAPTER SIX

They were on the sidewalk for an hour before they were let back into the building. As soon as they came back, they noticed the smell. Everyone ignored it at first, but a few hours later, when it wafted into Rebecca's office, she decided she needed to find out what was going on. As she walked into the bullpen, she saw Mindy stepped away from her desk, searching for the source of the odor as well. They both circled the office, receiving little comments of amusement from the resident workers. They wound up in the back of the room by the storage closet and looked at each other in confusion.

Rebecca was the first to the door and as she tried the knob, she realized it was locked.

"I'll get the keys," Mindy said as she turned and disappeared.

Rebecca was left staring at the door, wondering what was behind it that could have created such a putrid odor. Mindy returned and unlocked the door. Rebecca turned the knob and pulled the door open.

The influx of fresh air pushed the rank sulfuric tinged smell out of the dark closet and into the main room. It hit Rebecca like a brick wall and both she and Mindy were almost knocked off their feet. The rest of the room groaned and gagged in disgust. Many grabbed their garbage cans or ran for fresh air.

Rebecca's eyes watered as she looked into the closet and found the teddy bear she'd discovered in her office a few days before. It was collapsing from the inside out. She moved and shut the door. Mindy was still gagging in revulsion as Rebecca ran into the kitchen and grabbed some of the kitchen towels.

She returned and shoved them beneath the crack at the bottom of the door. She thought of what to do next and moved through the bullpen.

"Okay, everybody pack up, we're done for the day," she said to the remainder of the group. "Mindy, find anyone who isn't here and tell them they need to pack up and go home. We'll see everybody tomorrow."

She saw Mindy nod and move. Rebecca went to her office and called the building's security desk.

"Hi, this is Rebecca Gailen, in suite sixty-four ten. I need a security detail sent up, please," she said and heard the woman ask the nature of the problem. "Ah . . . we . . ."

It was then that she realized her hands were shaking and her stomach clenched as she attempted to breathe.

"We have a situation. Can you please just send someone up? Thank you," she hung up the phone and her stomach clenched again. This time it pushed out the contents of her stomach and she grabbed the garbage can by her desk.

Her head swam as she sat back in her chair.

This is not happening . . .

Keep it together, Rebecca, You can't lose it now, not yet . . .

Okay, Rebecca, focus.

She sat up, grabbed the phone and called her boss. She explained what happened and then the subsequent dismissal of the employees. He supported the decision. He proceeded to tell her that he trusted her, to be careful and to call if she needed anything. Rebecca thanked him for his understanding and hung up the phone with a small sigh as she rubbed the back of her neck.

"Everyone's gone," she heard Mindy say and as she jerked. "Sorry, I didn't mean to startle you."

Rebecca looked at her as she crouched beside her chair and covered her hand in concern.

"Are you okay?"

Rebecca managed a nod. "Yeah, I'm fine," she replied in a steady voice as she saw the security team she'd requested approach. "Security's here, I'll . . ."

"I've got it," Mindy insisted with a gentle smile. "You just sit for a couple minutes, okay?"

Rebecca nodded, helpless to argue with her and she exited the office. She watched her friend proceed to show the security team what they'd found. She rested her forehead on her hand and closed her eyes in complete exhaustion.

Why is this happening?

What does he want?

Mindy returned a few minutes later with a small smile as she closed the door to the office.

"What did they say?"

"They are calling the police. They should be here soon," Mindy said as she kept a steady reassuring gaze with hers. "Do you want to go get some fresh air before they get here?"

"No, I'm okay. I think I am getting used to it," she replied which made both of them giggle.

"I thought they were going to pass out when I opened the door," Mindy said which made Rebecca laugh a little harder. "It's a good thing I didn't take it to the hospital."

The comment hung in the air. Rebecca felt her shoulders shaking and realized she was crying.

"Oh God, Beccs," Mindy said as she crossed the room and pulled her into a warm hug. "It's gonna be okay. It is."

"I know. God, I feel like such an idiot."

"Hey, you need to use this to your advantage," Mindy said as she handed her a tissue. "There may be hot cops on their way and they're always a sucker for a damsel in distress."

Eric and Adam worked through another twenty-four hour shift and were in need of sleep. Adam talked on the phone as Eric headed up the stairs in desperate need of a pillow beneath his head. He wasn't sure what time it was, all he knew was that it was dark outside. He flopped down on the bed, not even bothering with his shoes. His mind fell into that place of silence and warmth, but continued its parade of thoughts, not acknowledging that he needed it to cease.

He pushed the nagging, disturbing reminders of his life away and began to drift. He searched for something soothing to latch on to. A flash of her amazing smile and brilliant eyes spawned a tidal wave of warmth and comfort to crash through him.

His entire being settled as he allowed himself to remember the way she felt against him. She remained nameless in his mind. No name he thought of suited her beautiful face. They'd had one amazing night, and he'd been unable to release the memory. Her eyes, her hair, even the scent of her skin lingered on him. He was reluctant to let them go. Her warmth still surrounding him, it pulled him low and coaxed him into a deep sleep.

The police arrived. Mindy and Rebecca both gave statements in regards to the delivery of the teddy bear and the events surrounding it. Overall, the officer Rebecca spoke to was very understanding and encouraged her to come to the station and file a full report.

They were hauling away the bear in a sealed plastic bag out the back when Rebecca saw Mindy enter the office, this time she didn't jump.

"You ready to head out?"

"Yeah, where's Charlie?"

"Waiting in the lobby for us," Mindy replied as Rebecca packed up her laptop. "Are you going to tell him what happened?"

"Do I have a choice?"

"I won't say anything if you don't want me to, Beccs," she offered with a small smile. "It's your call."

"I don't know . . . I just . . ." she replied with a deep sigh, already exhausted by the mere thought of the conversation. "Let's just play it by ear."

She hauled her bag over her shoulder and grabbed her purse. Mindy waited as she locked the door before they walked through the bullpen toward the lobby. Her gaze rested on Charlie as they turned the corner and instead of relief, her stomach clenched even more.

"Hey, Beccs," he greeted with a smile as she approached. "You ready for dinner?"

"Charlie, I'm sorry. I think I just want to go home," Rebecca replied. "It's been a long day."

"That's fine, you look tired, sweetie," he said with a nod as he rubbed her back.

"Are you sure?"

"Of course, I'll walk you ladies to your cars," Charlie said as he escorted them to the elevator.

Mindy pressed P3 and they were on their way. A few moments later, the doors opened and they stepped out. It was a little after seven and the sun had gone down. The garage was dimly lit and their footsteps echoed off the walls. They reached Mindy's car first, Rebecca's was two spaces away.

"Beccs, are you okay?" Charlie asked and she turned to face him.

"Yeah, I'm just tired," she replied as he reached out and pulled her into a hug.

"I'm going to follow you home, okay?" he said as he released her.

She turned and unlocked her car. "You don't need to . . ." she started as she pulled on the car door.

A rush of pressure erupted from inside the car. It pushed against the door and she lost her balance. Rebecca fell back and her legs were wet. She felt arms pull her out of the way as a rush of noise echoed off the walls. She turned, seeing dark water pouring out of her car.

"Oh my God!" Mindy cried as she moved toward them in alarm. She jumped back as chunks of something began to flow out with the liquid.

What is happening?

The liquid continued to flow from the car as Rebecca felt Charlie leading her away from it. She stared at the sight in confusion as Charlie pulled out his phone. She moved out of his arms and walked back to the car.

"Beccs, don't," Mindy called to her.

She ignored the plea, searching the liquid. It was then she realized what the clumps were as they scattered themselves on the concrete beneath her car.

Rats.

Drowned, dead rats.

"Stiles."

He heard someone calling him as he shifted in the bed, trying to ignore the attempt to wake him.

"Stiles."

Eric opened his eyes and looked toward the voice, seeing Adam at the door.

"Yeah?"

"Your brother's here."

"Alright, I'll be right there," he said with a groan as he shifted and rolled out of the bed. He shuffled to the bathroom and did a once over. He looked presentable although he felt like he was walking in a fog. He went to his desk and looked to Adam in question.

"He's downstairs with Lugow," Adam said.

Eric turned toward the stairs. Frank Lugow was the lead detective in the Domestic Violence and Stalking unit. They'd graduated in the same class at the police academy. He was a damn fine officer and Eric knew he would take care of whatever Charlie needed.

Eric reached the bottom of the stairs and saw his brother pacing in the waiting area.

"Charlie," Eric called to him and he turned as he approached.

"Hey, I uh . . . wasn't sure you were here. You didn't answer your phone so I called Adam."

"I was busy, what's going on?"

"The stalker I told you about. I was right when I said he was escalating."

"What happened?"

"Rebecca found a Teddy Bear in her office a few days ago. Her assistant stuck it in a closet and they forgot about it."

"So?"

"The toy was stuffed with entrails and God knows what else. It sat rotting in the closet until they found it this afternoon," Charlie explained as Eric took in his brother's panic. "Tonight when I came to pick her up for dinner, we went to her car. She opened the door and a flood of water and drowned rats spilled out. He filled her car with it, Eric. There were so many rats the water was red. He must've cut them open before he put them in."

"Okay, Charlie, you need to take a breath," Eric said as he tried to calm his brother down. "You brought her down. You did the right thing, now we can get involved and find whoever is doing this to her."

"This is so insane," Charlie said as he sat on one of the

chairs in disbelief. "I can't believe this is happening to her, Eric. She doesn't deserve this."

"Look, I know this is a tough situation, but these guys are the best. They will figure out what's going on and put a stop to it as soon as possible," Eric replied as he took the seat next to him. "Adam told me that Detective Lugow is talking to her?"

"Yeah, they've been in there about an hour now. He wanted to talk to her alone."

"It's going to be okay. You just need to be patient," Eric tried to reassure. "Do you want something to drink? I think there is some fresh coffee in the kitchen."

"Yeah that would be great, thanks," Charlie replied with a nod.

Eric got up and went to the kitchen. He went over the story in his head and wondered what his brother had gotten himself into. Lugow was the best though. If anyone could get to the bottom of it, he could. He went by the name Lug. Built like a refrigerator, he was 6'8, with brown hair, horn rimmed glasses and a head the size of a melon. You could always find Frank Lugow in a crowd.

Eric filled the cup, moved out of the kitchen and back to the waiting room. He saw Lugow talking to Charlie and two women who had joined him while he was gone.

"Stiles," Lug greeted as he joined them.

"Hey, how did it go?"

"Good, really good. We have a lot to go on and hopefully we can find this idiot fairly fast," he replied with a nod to Charlie in assurance. "I spoke to Rebecca about a safety plan and gave her some information about the local support and victims advocate group . . ." Lugow continued to explain to Charlie, and the two women, one of which he assumed was Rebecca, what needed to happen and the best ways to keep everyone safe.

Eric's eyes lifted and the air disappeared from the room. The unforgettable ringlets of her deep red hair pulled him back to Dallas, and he thought he was dreaming. He watched in stunned realization as the conference room door closed and she walked toward them.

She was here, standing right in front of him.

Her electric blue eyes hit him like a Mack truck as they lifted. She looked distraught, exhausted and fragile. The fog of apprehension had dimmed the fire of her eyes, and he remained breathless in panicked confusion.

She stopped mid-stride and her face froze in shock. Her eyes had locked onto him. An unexpected look of vulnerability stared back at him, and he thought for an instant, she was going burst into tears.

"Beccs, are you okay?" he heard Charlie ask.

The openness of her expression disappeared as she turned to Charlie. His brother moved to meet her. She nodded as his arm encircled her waist and Eric's chest burned.

"There's someone I want you to meet. This is my brother, Eric. Eric this is Rebecca."

The shock and confusion he felt were reflected in her eyes, but nowhere else. She was the first to react as she reached her hand out to him.

"Hi, it's nice to meet you."

"Nice to meet you, too," Eric managed to say as he took her hand, squeezing it as his body burned, and he felt like he was suffocating.

"This is Mindy and Donna, Rebecca's best friends," Charlie introduced as Eric reached out, shaking Mindy's hand and then Donna's.

"And personal bodyguards," Donna offered as she shook his hand.

He smirked at the comment and watched as Donna stepped back. She wrapped her arms around Rebecca's shoulders and she seemed to relax a little.

"Eric is a detective with the Major Crimes Unit. He and Detective Lugow went to the police academy together," Charlie explained, oblivious to the undercurrent of electricity coursing through the two of them.

"We should get going," Mindy said as she looked at Charlie.

"Thanks again for everything, Detective Lugow."

Charlie extended his hand to the man as Eric forced his eyes away from Rebecca.

"Anything you need. Be safe and let me know if anything else happens," Lug said to Rebecca.

"Oh she will, believe me," Donna commented and Eric saw her friend give her a small reassuring squeeze.

"Nothing is too minor and it doesn't matter what time of day. You call me."

Rebecca nodded, her eyes still focused on the floor.

"Thanks again guys. Eric, I'll call you tomorrow."

Eric didn't reply, he just nodded and watched Charlie escort the three women from the station.

"You okay, Stiles?" Lug asked.

Eric brought himself back into the moment. "Yeah, just not enough sleep. If there's anything I can do to help, let me know," Eric replied as he looked at his colleague.

"I just might take you up on that," Lug nodded before he turned and walked away.

Her name is Rebecca.

Charlie's new girlfriend.

Chapter Seven

Rebecca sat in the passenger's seat of Charlie's truck, unaware of the world as it passed around her. Donna was following them in her car and Mindy had gone home. Her mind had been a flurry of confusion and panic all night and now this.

Why tonight?

Why there?

Why him?

"Beccs, you okay?" Charlie asked as he reached out, wrapping his hand around the back of her neck.

She straightened her spine and nodded.

"You sure?"

"Besides not knowing how I'm going to explain this to my insurance company, I'm good," she replied, trying to reassure him. He began to caress the side of her neck with his thumb before he reached for her hand.

Charlie had mentioned Eric several times before. He described him as a bit of a hardass, but loyal and willing to do anything for those he considered part of his life. She'd heard several stories from their shared childhood. Rebecca had been anxious to meet Eric, wondering about the man Charlie so admired.

When her eyes landed on his, she thought the stress of her life had become too much and she was hallucinating. Seeing him again had been something she'd wanted for weeks. The memory of the night they met had become her only real sanctuary.

In the moment, a flood of relief and hope swept over her. The man she'd dreamt about for the past month was standing a few feet away. Then it hit her that he was Charlie's brother. It was all she could do to remain calm and cool despite the raging panic in her mind.

"Are you sure you want to go home?" he asked.

She tried to push her racing thoughts to the side.

"Because you can stay with me tonight if you want."

"I know it sounds crazy, but I want to go home and sleep," she replied as she pushed her hair off her shoulder, knowing that Charlie's bed was the last place she needed to be right now.

He dropped the subject as they got closer to her house and pulled into the driveway.

"Thanks for the ride, I . . ." she started as he turned off the car.

"I'm going in with you to make sure you're safe, Beccs," Charlie insisted as he got out of the car with her. "Donna's not here yet and I'm not going to just let you walk into the house alone after what just happened."

Rebecca nodded and walked to her door, pulling out her keys. She unlocked the door and felt him put himself in front of her. He walked into the house first. She was touched by the sentiment and smirked a little before she followed him in. She flipped on the light and turned off the alarm.

He proceeded to walk through the house as she waited at the door and then returned as she laid her purse on the table next to the door.

"Everything looks okay," he said as she nodded, his eyes glowing as he looked at her. "Does anything look out of place?"

"Ah . . . no," she said, taking a brief look around the immediate area. "No, everything looks fine. Charlie, it's not that big of a deal, really. So I have to have the car cleaned, it sucks, but . . ."

"Rebecca, someone filled your car with water and dead rats. Your office had to be evacuated because someone sent you a teddy bear filled with—"

"Charlie, please . . ."

"You can tell me that it's not a big deal all you want, but I know it is," he commented as he moved toward her, his hands wrapping around her waist as he looked down into her eyes. "Whether you like it or not, I'm not going to stop worrying about you."

"Well Detective Lugow is on it now, so it's going to be okay, right?" she asked, Charlie's closeness making her feel anxious as Eric's face settled in her mind.

She adored Charlie. He was so good to her, but now her hesitation about her feelings for him intensified. She'd thought it would just take time to forget about what happened in Dallas, but now it was all she could do not to think about it.

About him.

The nameless extraordinary man who could take her away from herself with a single look. He'd ignited a need she didn't recognize, even after a month, his hold on her hadn't subsided. She started dating Charlie, but was unable to allow him to come too close. She kept this wonderful man at arm's length, incapable of looking at him without seeing . . .

The man I can't seem to forget has a name.

Eric.

Charlie's brother.

"Right," he replied with a small sigh as he continued to gaze through her. His hands wrapped in her hair before he leaned down and kissed her.

Rebecca moved back as their lips parted, but he didn't seem effected and a knowing guilt washed over her.

"Are you sure you and Donna are going to be okay here

tonight?"

"We'll be fine," Donna responded as she entered the house.

"I have Donna's scowl and the alarm system. I'll be fine."

"Okay," he replied as he nodded and pulled her toward him again, brushing her forehead with his lips. "You have my number if you need anything."

"Yes," she replied as he opened the door to leave. "We'll call you if anything happens, I promise."

"Turn on the alarm as soon as I leave."

"Definitely," she replied with a nod as he stepped out of the house. "Charlie?"

"Yeah?"

"Thanks again for everything," she said with genuine sincerity. "I don't deserve you."

"Yes you do," he replied with a small wave.

She shut the door, set the alarm and leaned against the door. Reminding herself that it was just a car. The police were involved now and things would get better. She was home and fine.

"You ready for bed?" Donna asked.

"Don, you don't have to stay . . ."

"Yes I do, so just stop right now," her friend insisted as she moved toward her and put her arm around her. "Come on, time for bed, Beccs."

She needed sleep. They turned the lights off as they went.

"Are you okay?" Donna asked her as they stopped in front of the guest room.

"Yeah, I'm just tired," she replied with a nod.

"Okay, get some sleep and we'll talk in the morning," Donna said in a mothering tone before she gave her a hug and waited as Rebecca walked to her room.

She needed sleep, but wanted a shower, and within a few minutes, she stood beneath the hot water. She was desperate to clear her mind of anything not having to do with the streams of water hitting her back. The look of relief and alarm on his face when they locked eyes at the police station clung to her.

Charlie.

He'd been so good to her and what does she do . . . she goes and sleeps with his brother. At the very least, she could say she didn't know it at the time. And Charlie was still just a friend then, they hadn't started dating. Not that it would make the truth any easier to hear when he did find out.

How the hell had this happened?

Somewhere someone was laughing at her.

It was one night and they both walked away, thinking that they would never see each other again. It happened, it was between them and it was over. There was no reason Charlie ever had to know. Unless, of course, Eric found it necessary to tell him. Even if he did, it might be for the best. Charlie wasn't meant to be with her and she knew that. She'd just been a wimp about sharing that truth with him.

Maybe that's what this was, perhaps it was a sign that she'd let this drag on long enough. She just needed to end it now before things got worse.

Rebecca dried her hair, changed into a pair of boxers and a t-shirt. She walked toward the bed and heard a beeping from the other room. Listening, she realized it was her phone and smirked, knowing it was Charlie checking on them.

She moved through the dark house to her purse and grabbed the phone. She opened the message.

I'll make you scream, Rebecca.

She let the phone drop from her hands as if it burned. She heard it clatter to the floor. She stepped back, choking on the air in her lungs. She pulled herself out of the initial shock and looked at the door of the spare room. She squared her shoulders and reached down, picking up the phone. Re-

reading the message again, she hit delete and it disappeared. She put her phone on vibrate, tossed it back into her purse and headed to bed.

She crawled in, pulled up the covers and turned off the light. Her mind spun a million miles a minute and no matter what she did, it wouldn't stop. She laid in the darkness, staring at the ceiling.

In the security of her warm bed, she allowed herself to remember that night in Dallas. She permitted herself to admit that seeing him had made her head reel. She'd played the scenario out thousands of times in her head. What would happen if she met him again? The scenarios never included her dating his brother.

Rebecca wondered how similar the two brothers were. Was Eric as kind and generous as Charlie? He seemed to her to be more brooding and soulful, but in reality, she didn't know. She and Lucy were polar opposites, was it the same for Charlie and Eric?

She turned on her side as she re-examined what little she knew of him before the current revelation. The knowledge seemed to be empathic in nature, more instinctual than factual. It sounded ridiculous, but if asked if she knew him, she could have said yes or no.

A detective.

It explained the hesitation she'd picked up on when they first met.

A detective that wanted to be a teacher.

She smiled at the statement, despite herself, but it dipped into remorse. She wondered if she'd ever see him in that way again. Their sudden but brief reunion changed everything, and for whatever reason, that broke her heart.

Rebecca chased her mind from seeing Eric, to Charlie, to work, to her admirer and back again. She glanced at the clock. It was five AM. She gave up on sleep with a sigh and rose from the bed. She changed into her running clothes, grabbed her iPod and headed out of the house.

She thought back to what detective Lugow said the night before and decided to take an alternate route around the neighborhood. In the back of her mind, she knew she shouldn't be running alone at all. Her hand gripped her small can of mace a little tighter, and she let her mind get lost in the music. The needed jog was uneventful and she returned to her house an hour later. She wondered how she was going to get through the day.

Coffee, lots and lots of coffee and maybe a Vault or two . . .

Rebecca started some coffee and dressed for work. She thought of the day ahead as she pinned back the last of her curls. Donna was giving her a ride to work. Once she got to the office, she could call for a rental car until she figured out what to do about her now ruined vehicle. Somehow she doubted her insurance company would cover the damage. She walked into the kitchen, seeing Donna dressed and reading a magazine at the counter.

"Good Morning," Rebecca greeted with a smile.

"Good Morning, you were up early," Donna commented, not looking up from her magazine.

"I guess."

"Hey, I need you to do me a favor."

"What's up?"

"You know I made all kinds of New Year's resolutions this year and I haven't kept one of them. So I was thinking. Next time you decide to go for a run at 5 AM, can you wake me up so I can go with you?"

"Sure," Rebecca replied, knowing full well that she had just been scolded by her best friend.

"Awesome," Donna replied with a grin. "We should get going. I think it is definitely a Starbucks morning."

"Agreed," Rebecca replied, her mind going blank as the room went fuzzy. "I just need to grab my bag."

"Beccs, are you okay," Donna asked, looking at her in

concern. "You're really pale. Maybe we should hang out here today?"

"No, I'm fine. I just have a headache and didn't get much sleep."

"Beccs . . ."

"Don, please?"

"After you."

The sunshine caressed his face and he breathed in the desert air. The tourists were steadily gathering in awe of the chaos. The regular police had arrived and now he was waiting for homicide. He wanted to see who would be examining his masterpiece.

The expected sedan pulled up and two men exited. The driver was a little over six feet tall, medium build. He was wearing suit pants, a white shirt and blue tie. The other was an inch taller, donned similar attire, but wore a dark trench coat. The two men crossed beyond the crime scene tape and disappeared into the motel room.

He turned out of the crowd, his mind's eye seeing the room as they entered. He'd laid her out on the bed, her face peaceful and serene. Her arms folded over her bare stomach. The slice across her neck would look painted on as it matched her red lace bra and panties.

She was magnificent and he'd given her a step above a sedative so she would feel no pain. He recalled how she purred in the height of passion and arched her back. Her hair cascaded toward the floor as he caressed her body. The cut was quick and even. Her muscles jerked and then calmed. He guided her body as the red river poured down her neck, over her shoulders and down the length of her back.

Her lips were still warm when he kissed her goodbye.

He turned and walked away, mentally debating where he wanted to go for breakfast. He decided on the Waffle House. He ordered his eggs over hard with wheat toast and two strips of crisp bacon. He arranged the glass of orange juice to sit on the left of his coffee above his fork.

He then pulled out the tattered pocket notebook and began making his list of supplies. There was work to be done. Delicate work that would need his full attention. His thoughts roamed over the task, his creative juices bubbling within his chest as he envisioned her eyes filled with fear. He then reached into his pocket for a small recording device. He looked at it before obtaining a small plastic case that held his earbud headphones. He plugged them into the recorder and then pushed one of the buds into his right ear before he hit play.

The door of the restaurant opened and the metal framed smacked against the chain of bells positioned just in front of it. A moment later, he felt movement in the seat across from him. He didn't need to look up to know the man who sat down was the perfect specimen of male narcissism. Colored pictures, small loops and balls of metal adorned his body while his shaved head hid the receding hairline that marked his ascending age.

He had closed his eyes, but could feel the man staring at him. The man picked up the unused earbud and listened to the recording. Within a second, he pulled back from the earpiece.

"You are a sick fuck, aren't you?"

"I believe you should have something for me?" he asked as he opened his eyes in amusement.

"Yeah," the man replied as the waitress delivered a plate of food to the table. He tossed a sealed envelope on the table before he swiped a piece of bacon off the plate. "How long is this going to take anyway?"

"It takes," he replied as he pushed the now contaminated food away. "As long as it takes."

"It shouldn't take that long. How hard is it to drive someone crazy? Hell, she's a woman, half the work is already done for you."

"The will of the mind is not easily broken. It must be chipped at until it shatters on its own. It takes an extreme testament of will, time and patience, Douglas."

"For which I have neither," he said as he rose from the table. "Here, two weeks. Oh, and Marco said not to forget to wear your gloves."

Chapter Eight

"Gotta love Burrito Wednesday," Eric commented as he took a seat in the booth across from Charlie for the bi-weekly ritual they'd started in high school. Two years between them, they shared a lot of the same friends, but remained each other's best friend.

Designated to be a brother thing, Burrito Wednesday was a selected time for the two men to sit down and grunt back and forth while they ate. Some called it bonding. Eric and Charlie called it tradition.

"Did you go look at that place on Sundance?" Charlie asked, knowing that Eric was still hunting for an apartment.

"Yeah, the place was an overpriced dump," Eric replied as he took a bite of his arm-length Mexican delight.

"I figured you'd jump at the first place offered."

"Why would you think that?"

"You didn't seem too enthused to be staying with Dad."

"Nah, it's fine. I'm never there."

"True. Hey, I was wondering if you could—"

"Charlie . . ."

"Oh come on, Eric," Charlie objected in frustration. "We haven't heard anything since she filed the report."

It had been a little over a week since Charlie had brought Rebecca down to the station. Since then, as far as he knew, things had settled down. There had been no attempt at contact since the incident with her car.

With everything going on, Eric had done a good job of blocking Rebecca out of his mind. What happened between them was in the past. This was the present now, reality, and she was with Charlie.

"It's going to take time," Eric replied as he took a breath, eyeing the people around them. "Cases like these can take months, even years to solve. You are going to need to be patient."

"So I am just supposed to sit around when that thing is out there plotting a new way to terrify and maybe even hurt her?" Charlie replied.

The comment irritated him. "I can't wave a magic wand and make the guy appear or disappear! I wish there was another way, but there isn't. So you are going to have to deal with it like the rest of us."

"I don't like this at all."

"Join the club," Eric mumbled into his burrito.

"You don't understand. Rebecca is . . . well she's fiercely independent and if you ask me, in denial about the whole thing," Charlie tried to explain. "She's a moving target and I . . . I honestly don't know what to do."

"Look, Charlie, these things get intense and emotions run high. If you care about this girl, you need to step back and let it play out. Protect her, but don't force the issue. It is what it is. You have to realize that whatever this guy is planning, right now there is nothing you can do to stop him from trying. If anything, we need him to do something in order to catch him."

"So now she's bait?"

"That's not what . . . seriously, you need to chill out."

"I know . . . I know I do. I just . . . Eric, I really care about Rebecca," Charlie pleaded.

"I know you do and I am going to do whatever I can to help stop this."

I would never let anything happen to her . . . Her smile flashed in his mind and he pushed it away in annoyance at his own lack of control.

"Good, because I need a favor."

"What?"

"I have training starting Friday," Charlie said, referring to his work in the army reserve.

"Jesus, Charlie," Eric objected as his entire plan of avoidance shattered before his eyes. Knowing full well that training meant he would be gone for over a week. "No."

"I'm not asking for you to babysit her, just keep an eye on things while I'm gone."

"Charlie," Eric started to object and then in his mind saw Rebecca's distraught face at the station. "Fine."

"Good, thanks" Charlie replied as Eric took a huge bite of his neglected burrito. "Did you see Dad's plans for adding onto the back of the house?"

"Really? Where the hell is he going to get the money for that?"

"Oh that's the best part. He's going to do it himself."

"Aww shit," Eric replied as he looked at his burrito. "I'm going to have to get this to go."

"Why?"

"I need to go put a deposit down on that place on Sundance," Eric replied with a straight face and Charlie laughed.

"You're not serious," Rebecca asked as she sat on the floor beside the couch. "Did he really say that?"

"Yes, I swear to God that is exactly what he said," Mindy exclaimed before taking a sip of her martini.

"So what did you say back?" Donna asked, her slim, long body laid out on the couch across from Rebecca.

"What was I supposed to say?"

"Oh God, Min, what did you say?" Rebecca replied in

giggling dread.

"I told him to meet me in the supply closet."

"No you didn't!" Donna exclaimed as Mindy nodded.

"Oh jeez, I'm never going to be able to go in that closet again."

"Oh please, you never go in the supply closet now."

"And now you know why."

The three women had become friends through work. Donna was a client of theirs. She'd called their firm several years ago. Rebecca was just a staffing manager then and Donna's company needed a new systems analyst. Rebecca fulfilled the request and as a follow-up, she took Donna to lunch. From that fateful day on, there was a click and Rebecca knew she'd found a friend she'd have for the rest of her life.

Rebecca introduced Donna to Mindy and since then, the three of them were inseparable. While Rebecca adored Mindy, there was something unique about her relationship with Donna. She could read her like a book, and Rebecca couldn't keep a secret from her for long if at all. She was more than a friend. She was her sister in the purest sense of the word.

"If you ask me, you could use a little supply closet action, Beccs," Donna added. "I'm sure Mindy could hook you up."

"No thank you," Rebecca replied as the other two girls laughed aloud at her blush. "I'm doing just fine on my own."

"Oh yeah, Charlie," Donna replied with a twisted grin. "How is Charlie anyway? I thought you were going to put that to rest."

"Yeah," Mindy sighed in over exaggeration. "I have been waiting an awfully long time for you."

"Anxious to pick up the pieces, Min?" Rebecca asked with a smirk, knowing full well that Mindy had a huge crush on

Charlie.

"Someone has to."

"Be good, Charlie is a nice guy," Rebecca warned, remembering his eyes looking down at her in concern.

"Oh I see, Charlie is a *nice guy*," Mindy repeated, looking to Donna with a nod.

"Oh, a *nice guy*. Well, that explains everything."

"What does that mean?"

"Beccs, I hate to tell you, but all you meet are nice guys," Donna explained. "You attract them like a magnet. They all fall in love with you, things are good for a while and then the charm wears off. On your side, not theirs."

"That's not true."

"Yeah, honey, it is," Mindy replied. "But don't feel bad, we get it. You want a nice guy, but they just don't do it for you."

"You've discussed this?"

"At length," Donna replied.

"You're both insane," Rebecca replied, unable to suppress the giggle in her chest. "What's wrong with wanting a nice guy?"

"There is absolutely nothing wrong with wanting a nice guy, if you actually want one."

"But you don't," Mindy said, taking a sip of her drink. "Want one, I mean."

"What you want is a fiery bastard who holds you down and won't let you go," Donna replied with an added drama of falling back into the couch. "Figuratively speaking, of course."

"So you think I want some . . . some bad boy?"

"Not necessarily a bad boy per se," Mindy replied in clarification. "But someone with some strength. Someone who makes you weak in the knees, and makes your insides quiver with a look."

"Oh please, now I know you're insane," Rebecca objected again. The memory of Eric's gentle but demanding lips on hers in the hallway at the hotel made a heat rise in her neck. Shaking her head, she got up from the floor and walked into the kitchen.

"Why does that sound so insane to you, Beccs?" Donna asked, following her.

"Because he, or it, or whatever doesn't exist," Rebecca replied as she placed her empty martini glass on the counter and turned, grabbing the pitcher. "You're saying I want something that doesn't exist!"

"No we're not, Beccs," Mindy replied, joining them. "We just . . ."

"Look all we're saying is that you need to let go a little, walk on the wild side. Try something or someone new. Someone not so sweet."

"Okay who? Give me an example of someone who fits this criteria?"

"Uh well . . ." Donna replied as she struggled with the request.

"Ha! See you can't . . ."

"Wait, I have someone," Mindy exclaimed.

"Who?" both Donna and Rebecca asked at the same time.

"Detective Eric Stiles!"

"What?" Rebecca exclaimed in confusion, willing back the blush that threatened to erupt onto her cheeks.

"Oh yeah, good call, Min," Donna congratulated with a knuckle knock as she looked at Rebecca.

"Seriously . . ." she asked, trying to hide her heart pounding in her chest.

"He's hot, Beccs."

"Him, yeah definitely him," Mindy said in glee. "He has combustion written all over him."

"Combustion, really?" Rebecca questioned. She looked at

her in disbelief that she used that word to describe him and Mindy nodded.

"Denial is the first stage," Donna commented.

Rebecca laughed at Mindy while she made exploding motions with her hands. "You're both certifiable," Rebecca laughed, still looking to Mindy.

"Why, because we want you to be happy?" Donna asked.

"You don't want me to be happy, you want me to get laid," Rebecca replied with a laugh to mask the suffering of the dull ache of desire as she relived the night in his arms. She hadn't told anyone, not even Donna and Mindy about what happened in Dallas. Much less that the other party involved was Eric Stiles.

"And is that so horrible of us?"

"Really, Beccs, you could use a little . . . you know . . ."

"That is not true!"

"It's so true!"

"So you think I'm uptight?"

"Sweetheart, you're wound tighter than a pink piglet's tail," Donna replied, causing laughter to erupt from all three of them.

"A pink piglet's tail . . . seriously that's what you came up with?" Rebecca asked, hearing her home phone ring.

"Give her a break, it's the cheap booze talking," Mindy replied and the three of them continued to laugh as Rebecca picked up the phone.

"Hello," she greeted and heard nothing. The girls were still laughing aloud so Rebecca closed her ear to hear better. "Hello, is there someone there?"

Rebecca waited and then heard breathing. A chill slid up her back and she hung up the phone. She slammed it onto the cradle which got the other girls' attention.

"Who was that?" Mindy asked

The phone rang again and Rebecca jumped back. Donna

saw her reaction and picked up the phone. Rebecca watched and waited.

"Who is this, you *sick fuck!*" Donna yelled into the phone. "If I ever find out who the fuck you are, I'll fucking rip your balls off. *Leave her alone!*" Donna slammed the phone down and looked at Mindy and Rebecca.

They all waited and the phone rang again. Donna went for the phone and Rebecca reached out, pushing the speaker and the record button on the phone. They heard the breathing and then a woman started screaming at the top of her lungs, making all three women jump. Mindy backed into the corner. Donna stared down at the phone, her face pale. They listened to the woman wail like she was being cut open. Rebecca crossed the kitchen, grabbed her cell phone and dialed 911.

Rebecca reached the dispatcher when the screaming stopped and they all continued to stare at the phone, waiting for something to happen. After a moment, they heard a click and a dial tone. Donna hung up the phone and Rebecca gave the police her address.

Chapter Nine

Eric pulled out the cream and the followed it with fresh coffee. Returning to his desk, he focused on the stack of files in front of him and got to work.

An hour later, his desk phone rang.

"Detective Stiles."

"Stiles, you busy?" Lug asked.

A pit dropped into his stomach. "Ah, I guess not, what's up?"

"Can you come downstairs, I need to ask you something."

"Sure, I'll be down in a minute," Eric replied as he hung up the phone. He rose from his desk as his mind began to whirl in apprehension. Had something happened to Rebecca? Lug wouldn't have called him without a good reason. He headed down the stairs, reminding himself that he didn't care for her in that way. They would be talking about a case and a victim. Nothing more.

He stepped onto the DVSU floor and looked for Lug who waved him over to a conference room

"What's up?" Eric asked as he approached and Lug motioned for him to enter the room, closing the door behind them.

"Charlie asked that I call you if anything happened while he was gone."

"Something happened?"

"Yeah," Lug replied with a deep sigh as he turned to the table and pushed the play button on a media file.

Eric waited and then heard frantic screaming coming

from the computer.

Lug let it play for a few more seconds and then stopped the recording.

"What is that?"

"It's the recording from a call Ms. Gailen received yesterday evening," Lug replied as he looked at him.

"Wow."

"It gets worse."

"How?"

"I am not one-hundred percent sure, but it sounds like the recording is authentic."

"So someone is actually . . ."

"Yeah, I think so."

"Wait," Eric started, his mind reeling as the scenario took on a whole new face. "So what exactly are you dealing with, Lug?"

"I'm not entirely sure, that's why I wanted to talk to you," he replied as he looked at his colleague. "How well do you know Ms. Gailen?"

"I don't . . ." Eric started, realizing that despite the single amazing night, he was telling the truth. He didn't know her at all. "I don't know her. She's Charlie's friend."

"Friend or girlfriend?"

"I am . . . I'm not sure, girlfriend I guess. I honestly don't know," Eric replied as he scolded himself for the stumble.

"Okay, I'm going to package all of this up and send it over to Brewster," Lug said with a nod.

Eric continued to struggle with the situation. Brewster was the best profiler in the state and he could give Lug something to go on.

"I'll let you know as soon as I hear anything."

"Lug."

"Yeah?"

"Is she okay?" Eric asked, attempting to mask his hesitation at revealing too much.

"She's scared, but resilient," he replied with a nod. "Stubborn. She's doing okay. From what I can tell, her friends, Mindy and Donna, are taking good care of her. After this happened, I told her to take a vacation from her house for a little while. I think she is staying with Donna."

"Good," he replied, his thoughts racing. "I'll call . . . I'll call Charlie and let him know. Keep me in the loop?"

"Always."

"Thanks."

Rebecca rubbed the back of her neck as she wished her throbbing head away. She'd read the same email five times and still had no idea what it said. Two days after the phone call, and despite her friend's layer of protection around her, she was unable to close her eyes without hearing the screaming of the woman on the phone.

Okay, Beccs, you need to focus on work.

Work will make it all go away . . .

She went back to the email once more. There was a knock at her door and her entire body clenched in terror at the noise. She looked up, seeing Mindy in the doorway with two cups of coffee in her hands.

"You're truly a goddess," Rebecca said, forcing a grin as Mindy approached.

"Can I have a raise?"

"Sorry, not my department, but I can put the good word in for you."

"That's all I ask," she replied as Rebecca attempted to take a sip of her coffee, but her hands trembled and she put it back on the desk.

"How are you doing?"

"I'm great," she replied with a smile as her friend looked at her with incredulous eyes. "I am, really. Go file or something, will you? Hovering is very unflattering."

"Well on that note, I'm going to go have some closet fun. I'll be back."

She laughed out loud.

Mindy walked out of the room.

Rebecca went back to work and was able to accomplish something for a change. She became engaged within a very large complex spreadsheet and barely heard her phone when it rang.

"This is Rebecca."

"Beccs?"

"Charlie!"

"Hey, I had a couple minutes of standing around before we leave and thought I'd give you a call."

"Sounds like you're checking up on me," she said. She knew Charlie would be out of town for a while on reserves duty and couldn't help but feel a little relieved by it. She was coming unhinged. Adding Eric into the fold, she didn't need him thinking she was crumbling, even if she was.

"Maybe a little of that, too."

"Uh-huh," she replied as she leaned back into her chair. "I know you have better things to do, Charlie. Really, you don't have anything to worry about, I'm fine."

"Yeah well I just don't think you should have to deal with this alone, Beccs," he replied, sounding frustrated with her.

"So are you staying safe?"

"Safe and sound," he replied. "How about you?"

"Yeah, of course," she replied with a wince of guilt. "Work has been crazy, but besides that, it has been quiet."

"Good," he replied. "Oh, hey, I have to go. Eric will be around if you need anything, Beccs."

"Okay, but everything is fine."

"Promise me you'll call him if anything happens."

"Charlie."

"Promise."

"Fine, I promise," she replied with her fingers crossed. "Be safe."

"Thanks, bye, Beccs."

"Bye, Charlie," hanging up the phone, her mind flashed to Eric and a feeling of warmth pooled in her stomach. She pushed it away.

Combustible . . . .danger.

I need to get him out of my head now.

She needed caffeine. Rebecca picked up her coffee cup without looking and realized it was empty. She rose from her chair to get more when her head swam in static and grabbed for her desk. It took a minute to pass, but it did and she headed to the kitchen.

She passed Mindy's desk and could see she was dragging as well. Rebecca grabbed her cup off her desk as Mindy smiled while talking on the phone and going through a stack of mail.

Rebecca pulled the cream out of the fridge and realized it was almost empty. They'd gone through a lot of coffee. Her head began to swim again and she reached for the counter to steady herself.

She needed to sleep.

She was aware of this fact, but it seemed unattainable. Standing here, she could close her eyes and fall asleep for a little while. At home, in her bed, or even at Donna's, her eyes refused to close. It was as if her brain was afraid she'd miss something important. Maybe she would try some of that pain medicine with the sleep agent. With any luck, it would knock out her headache and make her sleep at the same time.

She filled both cups and replaced the pot on the burner. She picked up her mug, blowing on it before taking a sip. As the hot coffee hit her lips, an ear-piercing scream echoed into the small kitchen. Rebecca's heart leapt in fear as the mug dropped from her hands and she ran out of the kitchen.

Mindy sat at her desk, screaming in horror. She looked at Rebecca and then stood, revealing her blood-covered hands and clothes.

"Mindy!" Rebecca said as she ran to her friend's side.

The surrounding bullpen began to gather, gaping in horror as Rebecca turned Mindy's panicked face toward her. "Mindy, breathe, sweetie, are you hurt?"

"No, I . . . .I . . ." she said as she began hyperventilating.

Rebecca felt someone hand her a bag. "Just breathe and tell me what happened," Rebecca said again.

Mindy burst into tears as she began to breathe into the bag.

"Allison, can you please walk her to the bathroom? I'll be there in a minute."

"Sure," Allison, one of the payroll processors, replied as Rebecca helped Mindy out of her chair and led her to Allison's side.

"I'll be right there," Rebecca said as Allison and Mindy disappeared from view.

As soon as they did, she commanded the rest of the staff back to work. They turned in whispers and stolen glances, but she didn't care. She tore over Mindy's desk in search of the source of the blood. Something bumped against her foot. She looked down, seeing an express box standing upright on the floor.

Rebecca grabbed a tissue and picked up the box. She adjusted the desk light so she could peer inside, but she couldn't see anything. She pulled the desk lamp above the package and saw that the box was lined with plastic. Settled at the bottom of the package was a pool of black liquid.

Someone sent me a box of blood?

Her gaze rose to see if the office was watching her and saw a flurry of movement. She took the box into her office and propped it against the side of her desk. She exited the office and locked the door behind her. She decided what to do next as she headed to the bathroom.

Allison was still trying to get Mindy to stop crying as Rebecca opened the door. Mindy looked up and walked to her in tears. She gave her a friend a hug while trying to calm her down. After a few minutes, Mindy began to breathe like a normal person. Allison washed the blood off her colleague's hands while Rebecca stayed close.

There was a knock on the door and they heard a familiar male voice. Mike, their friend from IT, and Mindy's closet buddy, stepped into the bathroom. As soon as he looked at Mindy, she burst into tears again. He moved to her, enveloping her in his arms, and she buried herself within his embrace.

Rebecca's watched the display of affection and her stomach felt hollow and cold. She didn't expect the wave of emotion that swept through her as Mindy relaxed within the man's embrace.

"Will you take her into one of the conference rooms and sit with her until the police arrive?" Rebecca asked Mike, and he nodded before she left the bathroom. The walk back to her office was longer than she imagined as she fought against the welling need to lose control. She unlocked the door, and once again bit back the need for emotional release. Pushing it down into her stomach, she took a breath and cleared her mind.

She dialed Detective Lugow's number and then Donna's.

Eric's phone buzzed and he pulled it out as he hit print on his computer.

"Detective Stiles."

"Stiles."

"Did something happen?"

"Yeah," Lugow answered.

Eric looked at his watch. "Where are you?"

"Her office, 6342 Jones, suite 6410."

"Okay, I'm on my way," he said as he let Adam know he was taking off.

Eric walked into the office forty-five minutes later and found Lugow talking with several security guards and a frustrated suited man. He scanned the room for Rebecca. Instead, he saw Donna talking to someone in one of the offices. He approached, still not sure what he was doing there.

"Beccs, you need to stop. This was not your fault!"

"The box was meant for me and she opened it! How can it not be my fault, Don?" Rebecca replied in anger.

He watched her push her hand through her hair in frustration.

"Detective Stiles, thank God. Can you please help me talk some reason into her? She is insisting that all of this is her fault," Donna said as he looked at Rebecca.

She turned to face him, held his gaze for a moment and then looked away. He tried to think of something to say, but he had nothing. Saved by the bell, so to speak, Donna's phone rang and she excused herself from the room.

Eric watched Donna go and realized this was the first time he'd been alone with her since . . .

"You don't need to be here," Rebecca said in a low tone as she walked to what he assumed was her desk. "I appreciate the gesture, but I'm . . ."

She was about a foot away.

His gaze followed her as she tried to act busy. He moved toward her and when she turned again she was inches from him. His body hummed with her proximity as the sweet scent of peaches seeped into his pores. He locked her wide eyes, almost forcing her to look at him. "Rebecca, it's not your fault." Her eyes seemed to soften as he said it, and he watched her take a broken breath of air.

"We are all done here, Rebecca," Lugow said, his voice breaking into the office.

Eric saw her jump in fear.

"I am going to have a squad car follow you home."

"I got it Lug," Eric said and she turned away from him again.

"Did I hear that we're done?" Donna asked as she joined the group.

"Yeah," Lug answered. "You are going to your place?"

"Yep."

"I need to talk to Jim before I go, if you'll excuse me," Rebecca said as she exited the room.

Eric watched as she walked across the office and stopped to talk to the suited man.

"Detectives," he heard Donna say and both men turned their attention to her. "Thank you for everything you are doing, but how do we make this stop? Beccs is very good at putting up a brave front. I don't know how much more of this she can take."

"We are doing everything we can to find the man or person who is doing this."

"I know you are. My gut is just telling me that there's more going on here than we know. I also have a hunch that you're thinking along the same lines."

"We are looking into all of the possibilities," Lug answered in a very even diplomatic tone.

"Look, Beccs takes care of herself and everyone else. She's not used to anyone taking care of her, nor does she really allow it. She thinks it makes her weak," Donna explained as Eric glanced at Rebecca still talking to the suited man. "She won't play the victim even when she should. So, this needs to end sooner rather than later. Especially now that it has affected someone other than her."

"Why do you say that?" Eric asked.

"Now that this freak is threatening someone other than her, she'll put herself in the line of fire to catch him," Donna explained as both men looked at her in alarm. "I'm going to do my best to keep her under wraps, but the sooner this ends the better."

"We couldn't agree more."

"Good. That being said, I'm going to take her home and put her to bed before she falls over. Detective Stiles, you will be escorting us home?"

"Indeed," Eric replied, impressed with the woman's tenacity.

"Terrific, let's go."

"Everything looks good," Eric said with a nod. "If anything happens don't hesitate to call."

"We won't, thank you, Detective," Donna said as she glanced at Rebecca and then walked away.

"Do you need anything?" he asked as he looked at Rebecca, who remained beside the door. She had taken the position when they arrived and hadn't moved.

"I'm fine," Rebecca said as she pulled her gaze from its focus on the floor to look at him.

Her usually brilliant eyes were dull and distracted, and he found himself searching for something to say to her. His chest ached to touch her, but he refused himself the want, relenting instead to the logical reaction for his presence.

"Thanks for coming," she said to him in a flat even tone as her eyes drifted.

He nodded, with a deep breath, taking note that it was the second time she'd been the first to break the silence, "My pleasure." He struggled to keep control and took a very abrupt step to the door.

The movement seemed to pull her out of her mind and

she met his gaze.

"Keep the doors locked and let Donna answer the door," his mouth said, his body filled with pain and panic in the same moment.

"Thanks," she said and opened the door as he stepped onto the porch.

He looked back as she closed the door.

She disappeared and a chill ran through him as if all the warmth had disappeared from the air. He moved on autopilot and walked back to his truck. He looked at the apartment, saw the lights dim and he was able to take a breath.

Eric stepped through the door of his father's house and watched as his father walked out of the kitchen in surprise.

"Is everything okay?"

"Yeah, why?"

"It's before two," his father replied as he followed him into the kitchen.

Eric pulled out a beer from the fridge and took a seat at the table. "Adam's covering for me."

"Adam, how is Adam? Haven't seen him around much. I guess that baby of his is keeping him busy."

"That baby isn't such a baby anymore, Dad, she just turned two."

"Did she really?"

"Yep, Olivia and Adam are actually going to start trying for another one," Eric replied with a smile as he watched his father lean against the counter, drinking his coffee. It was his usual position and almost a comfort to see how little changed when he wasn't around. "Have you talked to Charlie?"

"Yeah, he called me around dinner," his dad replied. "Sounds good. Well, he sounds good for being at war."

"He's not at war, Dad," Eric defended. "He's in the

reserves."

"The reserves go to war just like the rest of them."

"Charlie finished his tour. He'll be home for a while."

"Not if he has anything to say about it," his dad replied in loving irritation. "If they called him back to active duty, he'd go."

"Dad . . ." Eric tried to interject on Charlie's behalf.

Their father was somewhat a pacifist, having grown up in the sixties, and while he was proud of his sons, he didn't always agree with their choices. One of the blotches on Charlie's record as a model son was his joining the Army.

When the country went to war, he felt it was his duty to defend it. It was noble and naïve, but it was Charlie. He'd done what he needed to do and came back alive, which is what mattered. He stayed active in the reserves as a way to keep a steady cash flow cushion for the bar.

"Although I'm not so sure that is true anymore. I've noticed a change in him. I think he's looking for the one."

"The one?"

"Yeah, not that you would know anything about settling down at all," his Dad jabbed at him. "I won't see any grandkids out of you until hell freezes over or I'm dead."

"I wouldn't go that far."

"Oh, a glimmer of hope?"

"I didn't say that."

"So you are reinforcing my point then?"

"Come on, Dad, in my line of work what's the point in trying to act like you have a normal life when you don't?" Eric explained as he followed his Dad into the living room. "You see how it is. I'm gone all the time. I don't have any set schedule and I don't know where I'm going or what I'm doing day to day."

"Excuses. You could change that if you wanted to."

"It's not that easy."

"If you wanted to, you could."

"Fine, Dad, I don't want to, and I don't see how that is going to change."

"There is more to life than a job, Eric," his Dad replied as he took a seat in his easy chair.

"Dad . . ." Eric started with a sigh, tired of having this same conversation with his father.

Eric's entry into the police academy wasn't so much a blotch as it was a grumble under his father's breath. His one saving grace was that he remained close to home.

"I know you're tired of this conversation, but I worry about you, son," his dad offered. "What happens when the job isn't what it once was for you? What will you have then? I'm just afraid of you ending up alone."

"If that's what happens, it's what happens."

"Your mother gave me enough love to last a lifetime and she's always with me even in death," his dad replied. "I would really like you to be able to say the same."

"What you and Mom had was special. The chances of me finding someone like that are one in a million."

"Just do me one thing."

"What?"

"Promise me that if she does come along you won't walk away."

"What if I don't know what I'm walking away from?"

"What do you mean?"

"How am I supposed to know if . . . she's the one?"

"You'll know, trust me, you'll know."

Eric caught up on the sports highlights and went to bed an hour later. As soon as his head hit the pillow, his mind fell on the events of the day as it did every night. The exception being now it seemed to start with Rebecca and ended with . . . Rebecca.

His father's words rang in his ears. The man made it seem

so easy. You find the woman you're meant to be with, you settle down, have a few kids and a dog. Life is wonderful. Eric just couldn't see that in his future, he wasn't even sure if it was something he wanted for his future.

He wasn't unhappy with his life the way it was now. He did what he wanted, when and if he wanted. There were no strings, no conflicts, no one to leave behind. He already had enough people depending on him. He didn't need to add to the bunch.

The night he'd spent in Dallas was the first time anything was ever his. There was no back-story, no mutual friends and no reasons to hesitate. It was one perfect night that was his. For that one night there was no job, no family and no life. It was just her eyes and the way he needed her.

She was Charlie's girl now and the illusion was shattered. Her eyes weren't just his anymore. Once again, he was forced to share with his brother. The phrase *I saw her first!* came rushing to his mind and he couldn't help but chuckle.

If only it was that easy.

You can make it happen if you want it to.

Did he want to? Did he want to open that door of a real relationship with a commitment, responsibility and someone else expecting something out of him? He'd had enough of that. He'd walked away from it numerous times. It worked for people like Charlie and his dad, but it wouldn't work for him. It wasn't in him to give himself up to something that domestic. He'd tried before and all he ended up getting was an empty apartment or a penniless bank account.

She'd expect him to be there for her, she deserved to have someone who could take care of her and support her. She deserved a normal life filled with everything she wanted. He could never give her that. He didn't want to be the one she relied on to make her happy.

Eric mulled the thoughts and fell into a deep sleep.

Snow, there was falling snow, but he wasn't cold. He was warm and shrugging his shoulders, he felt the softness of a heavy sweater against his arms.

Where was he?

"It's cold out there," he heard Charlie's voice say and he turned, facing him.

"Good thing we're inside," Eric heard himself reply and took the moment to look around. The room was bathed is warm colors, wood and stone. A crackling fire to his right was surrounded by worn leather couches covered in thick blankets.

"Daddy, can we go outside and see the horses?" he heard a small girl's voice echo as she ran into the room.

"Abby, it's too cold, sweetie. Maybe tomorrow," he heard Rebecca's voice say as she entered the room, carrying a tray of cups.

"Oh all right," the little girl said as she followed Rebecca to the table, reaching for a cup. Rebecca sat on the couch, smiling at the child as she pointed out the cup with the whipped cream.

Eric moved to the couch, taking a seat beside the child as he continued to watch Rebecca and Charlie. Charlie was talking on the phone off in the corner. Rebecca looked up at him with a gentle smile.

"Do you want marshmallows or whipped cream?" Rebecca asked him.

"Uh, I don't care," Eric replied, startled by the question.

"You have to pick one, Uncle Eric!" the child said as he felt a stab of disappointment.

"Yeah, Uncle Eric, choose," Rebecca supported as she met his eyes with a small grin.

"How about you choose for me?" Eric asked the child as he took a deep breath.

"Mallows!"

"Mallows it is," Eric said as he nodded to Rebecca and she plopped a few in his cup. The child heard something he didn't and went running out of the room. Eric saw Rebecca picking up her cup and he turned to the fire, his chest heavy with regret.

He felt someone on the couch next to him. Rebecca appeared, covering them both with the blanket as she curled her legs beneath her and sat down. She lifted his arm as she snuggled into him, her head resting against his chest.

The warmth that came with her embrace was unimaginable and his arms pulled her closer into him as he kissed her forehead.

"Uncle Eric, Aunt Beccs, Mommy's here!" the little girl yelled as she ran into the room in excitement. Eric and Rebecca both acted surprised, laughing as she jumped on them.

Eric's eyes opened and he was staring at his clock. He closed his eyes again and reveled in the warmth from the dream that still surrounded him. He could see her smiling at him, her hair shining in the light of the fire.

Could it ever be that perfect?

Lying in the wake of the dream, his heart said it could. Remembering the warmth of her touch, there was nothing in the world he wanted more than to hold her against him and never let her go.

Chapter Ten

R ebecca walked into the conference room and took a seat at the corner of the table facing the window. She opened her bottle of water and took a sip as she stared out into the bright blue sky. She wished for a day where the worst she had to worry about was a presentation or returning a stack of phone calls. Instead, she was frantic with fear and dread over what was waiting for her outside these four walls. She wanted her life back, it may not have been perfect, but it was hers.

Someone asked her a question and she was brought back to the conference room. She realized the meeting had begun around her and she hadn't noticed. She collected herself and, focusing on the task, got through the meeting and met Mindy outside as planned.

"Did you send the changes to Annie?"

"Yes."

"Any messages?"

"No . . . well . . . no."

"What does that mean?"

"We got a couple of heavy breathers," she started and Rebecca began to object. "But nothing for you to worry about. I called Lugow and he is calling the phone company."

She walked into her office and shut the door. She took the time to catch up on emails and became wrapped up in her own mind. A loud rapping on the door startled her and taking a breath, she walked to the door, opening it.

"Hey," Donna greeted.

"Hey, what are you doing here?" Rebecca greeted with a smile as she moved to her desk and looked at her laptop.

"I was down the street and I wanted to stop by and see how you were doing," she said as she moved into the office and closed the door.

"I would be great if everyone would stop asking me that. Besides the minor fact that Mindy was the one who opened the box of blood, not me."

"Beccs, calm down. I talked to Mindy, she's fine," Donna replied, her voice flat and calm. "You had a rough night last night. I know you didn't sleep and . . ."

"So I didn't sleep. Shit happens," she snapped and then pulled back. "I'm sorry, Don, I just . . . I just want it to stop."

"I know you do," she agreed with a patient nod. "You do realize in order for that to happen you're going to have to tell Detective Lugow and Detective Stiles everything that's going on."

"Detective Lugow is the officer on my case," she corrected. "I've told him everything he needs to know."

"Beccs . . ."

"I am not going to drag her into this. This is hard enough without that as well!"

"Okay, let me ask you this, is there any way that the two are related?"

"No."

"Are you absolutely sure?"

"No."

"You need to tell him, Beccs," Donna advised despite her protesting. "You can trust them. They're trying to help you."

"I can handle it," she insisted, sounding ridiculous even in her own mind.

"Rebecca, come on, not even Erica Kane could handle what's been going on in your life," Donna replied with a chuckle. "It's okay to ask for help you know."

"I know that, I just . . ." she replied and then struggled with her conflicted emotions. "I just don't want it from him."

"Who?"

"No one."

"Detective Stiles," Donna replied, looking at her in suspicion. "What's your deal with this guy?"

"There's no deal."

"Beccs, come on."

"What?"

"It's me, your best friend, I can see right through you. What's going on with Detective Stiles that you aren't telling me?"

"Just drop it, it doesn't matter anyway."

"I'm not going to just drop it."

"Please?"

"Fine," Donna replied. "But you will tell me. You know that right?"

"Yes."

"So I was talking to Mindy and we decided that she and Mike are going to—"

"What are you talking about?"

"Tonight."

'What about tonight?"

"You're not—"

"I wouldn't abandon you on your big night, Don!"

"It's not a big deal, maybe you—"

"No, I'm going and that's final. I'll have Mindy run me home to change and you can pick me up at the house," Rebecca replied, feeling good about the evening ahead.

While the awards dinner at Donna's firm was the furthest thing from her mind, she was looking forward to attending. Donna had worked hard over the past ten years. She deserved recognition for it and Rebecca wasn't going to miss it.

"See you then," Donna replied before she left.

Rebecca had a moment to breathe. Part of her wanted to tell Donna everything, if for no other reason than to have someone to talk to about this ridiculous mess.

Okay Beccs, get to work.

Focus.

Rebecca dropped her purse and bag by the door, and made a mad dash to the bedroom. She grabbed her do-it-all black dress from the closet. She stripped down and re-dressed before she moved into the bathroom. She looked at her reflection with a sigh. Thank God for makeup.

She covered the dark circles around her eyes, threw on some light blush, eye shadow and went back to her closet to look for a suitable clutch. She heard a loud bang. She froze and then headed out of the closet into her empty bedroom.

Mindy was busy with Mike so she decided that she would just run home, change and then drive to Donna's. She would be in and out. Not allowing enough time for anything to happen.

She felt a slow tremble erupting in the pit of her stomach as she stepped out into the hall. She looked around as she reached for the light switch. The sun wasn't gone, but was low enough to cast odd shadows in the house. Seeing noth-ing, she peered into the kitchen and then another bang made her jump. Exhaling her held breath, she realized the bath-room window was open and the desert breeze was pushing against the blinds.

She hugged her arms to herself as she shook it off and walked back into the bedroom to resume her search. She found the clutch and her favorite pair of heels. She walked out of the bedroom when the doorbell rang and her phone beeped at the same moment.

Her entire body stiffened again and her heart stopped in terror. She forced herself to move and picked up her phone as she walked to the door. She saw she had a voicemail waiting for her. She checked out the peephole and saw nothing. She turned the knob of the door and opened it.

She heard the flapping of paper and realized it was a day marketer leaving her a flyer. Her voicemail began to play and she heard the screaming. She looked down in distress to find a large bouquet of roses sitting on the step in front of the door. Her tolerance burst. In an emotional rage, she kicked the vase as hard as she could. She watched as it flew upward and shattered against the concrete as it landed.

"Leave Me Alone!" she screamed into the orange night. Her phone rang in her hand again. This time it sent a shock of anguish through her. She proceeded to hurl it toward the street before she slammed the door shut.

Her heart pounded as she grabbed her clutch off the counter and ran from the house to her car. Without thought, fueled by her anger and fear, she peeled out of the driveway and down the street, realizing she couldn't breathe.

She hit the brakes and the car came to screeching halt. She smacked the steering wheel in frustration, still trying to re-cover from a lack of oxygen. Her head rested on the steering wheel in defeat. She closed her eyes and focused on her lungs expanding and contracting within her chest.

After a few minutes, she could feel her body accepting the air and, leaning back into the seat, she stared out the wind-shield. Able to focus, she put the car in gear and looked out to the street. Rebecca stopped as her heart stuttered in fear. She unfocused her eyes, seeing the rose attached to her wiper.

She put the car in park and got out in pure disbelief. Her eyes remained fixated on the windshield. Seeing that the rose wasn't a figment of her imagination, she reached out and pulled it from the windshield. Rebecca spun and searched the area. She found it calm, quiet and devoid of an-ything sinister. Her heart racing once again, she got back in her car. She tossed the rose to the side as she ignored the panic in her mind and the fluttering of darkness that threatened her consciousness. She put the car in drive, hit the gas and abandoned her fear in the street.

Rebecca arrived at Donna's apartment twenty minutes later. She climbed the stairs and reached for the doorknob when it opened.

Donna stood, staring at her in confusion.

"Hey," Rebecca greeted with the brightest smile she could muster as Donna closed the door and they headed down the stairs.

"Beccs, where —"

"You look fabulous."

"Thanks . . . so do you."

"So where are we headed?"

"Downtown."

"Great, lead the way."

They got in her car and headed out. Rebecca was happy for the momentary silence, but was also thankful for her friend's mere presence. Replaying the events in her head, she felt like an idiot. She destroyed evidence, tossed a perfectly good phone and freaked out in the middle of her neighborhood.

She needed to just forget about all of it, tonight was Donna's night. She deserved it and Rebecca wasn't going to let anyone ruin it.

She made up her mind, put on her party face and focused on Donna's happiness. They arrived at the awards dinner half an hour later. The cocktail hour had begun and Donna ordered them both cosmopolitans. After her second drink, Rebecca was feeling relaxed and was laughing with Donna and a crowd of her co-workers. Dinner service was shortly thereafter and then the awards were handed out. Donna was third in line and Rebecca clapped and cheered for her friend.

The awards ceremony ended and work friends surrounded them. The women laughed and drank until Donna pulled her phone out of her purse. She looked at it and gave Rebecca an odd look.

Donna took the call.

Rebecca scanned the crowd of guests, all now beginning to feel the effects of the alcohol they'd been consuming.

"Beccs."

She turned.

Donna held the phone out to her. "It's for you."

"What?" Rebecca replied in confusion as Donna watched her take the phone. "This is Rebecca."

"Stiles."

"Eric."

"Hey, bro, where are you?" he said, hearing Charlie's voice.

"It doesn't matter, when was the last time you talked to Rebecca?"

"I uh . . . Charlie . . ."

"Did you talk to her today?"

"Ah no . . . I don't—"

"Because I've tried to call her five times over the past two hours and she hasn't answered," Charlie replied as the call began to break up.

"She's probably out or asleep."

"No, she always picks up her phone or calls me right back."

"I saw her a few nights ago," Eric started, seeing the dimness of her eyes in his mind. "She's fine, you need to chill."

"Eric . . . need . . . wrong . . ." Charlie said as the phone continued to cut in and out.

"I'll call her, I'll make sure she's okay," Eric said into the phone, unable to know either way if Charlie could hear him. "Charlie?"

The call dropped and Eric growled in frustration as he typed a text to Charlie, letting him know he'd take care of it.

"Was that Charlie?" Adam asked as he straddled his chair, facing his desk.

"Yeah," Eric replied as he dropped the phone on the desk, debating what he should do next. Picking up the phone again, he dialed Rebecca's number. The phone rang a few times and then the voicemail picked up. "Rebecca, it's Er . . . Detective Stiles, call me."

"Who's Rebecca?" Adam asked.

Eric stared down at his phone. "Ah . . . nobody," he said and then called and left a message for Lugow before he went back to the files on his desk.

The two men worked for the next hour and while they'd made progress, his mind pulled to the fact that Charlie had called and Rebecca hadn't called back. Not that she would, considering the current situation.

The nagging of uncertainty got to him and unable to reach Lugow, Eric headed out of the office. He went to Donna's, finding the apartment vacant. Annoyed by the fact that he'd conceded to his brother's paranoia, his own concern for her began to overtake the irritation. Next he headed to her house, although why she would be there bothered him as much as her not being at Donna's.

Her car was missing as he pulled up to the house which he took as a good sign. He headed to the door and heard the sound of crunching glass beneath his feet. He glanced down and found a pile of scattered roses and a shattered glass vase. Eric's heart beat a little faster. He found the door of the house locked. He tried to look in through the bay window, but the drapes were closed, blocking his view. There weren't any lights on inside. He dialed her number again, hearing it ring and then go to voicemail. He dialed again and noticed the faint sound of a cell phone ringing in the immediate area.

He pulled the phone away from his ear as he listened for the sound again. It stopped and, listening to his own phone, he heard her voicemail kick in. He redialed her number as he moved down the yard. He pulled the cell away from his ear, listened again and heard the ringing of a phone across the street and to his left. He followed the sound until it stopped. He hung up and redialed her number again. His heart thudded in his ears as he moved toward the sound. Images of her hurt or worse flashed in his mind.

Eric heard the ringing just feet away and located the phone behind a bush. Picking it up, he wiped it off, seeing that she had eighteen missed calls. Several from him, Charlie, Donna and an *unknown number*. Donna's number was the most recent next to Charlie. He called her from Rebecca's phone, forcing himself not to panic.

"This is Donna."

"Donna, hey it's Detective Stiles."

"Detective Stiles, why are you calling me from Rebecca's phone?"

"That's what I'd like to know. When was the last time you to talked to her?"

"About ten seconds ago."

"Excuse me?"

"She's here with me," Donna replied.

A flood of relief washed over him.

"Is everything okay?"

"As far as I know, would you mind if I talked to Rebecca?"

"Not at all, hang on a sec," she replied.

He waited as he figured out what he was going to say to her. Looking back to the house, at that moment, he didn't want to know what happened or why her phone was in the bushes, he just needed to hear her voice.

"This is Rebecca."

His stomach unclenched and he allowed the relief to wash over him again. "It's Det . . . Eric," he said, waiting for her to say something, anything. "I found your phone."

"Really? I didn't know it was missing."

"Where are you?"

"I'm out with Donna," she replied. "Thanks for finding my phone, I need to go."

"Rebecca . . ." he started to object and then heard the call drop. He let the phone drop in his hand as he debated what he should do next. She'd had another visit from her friend.

Eric walked back to his truck as he typed a message to Charlie. He then called Lug and the crime lab to retrieve the shattered remnants of the flower arrangement. He hung up the phone and thought about going back to Donna's and camping out on the porch until they returned home. His phone beeped and he looked down to see a text waiting for him. It was an address from Donna's phone.

He got back into the truck and headed to meet them. He heard his phone beep again and he looked down to see a response from Charlie.

Thank you.

Exiting the message, his guilt laid in his stomach. Did he have any reason to feel guilty? He was doing what his brother asked by keeping tabs on Rebecca. That was what he agreed to do and that was all he agreed to do. If something happened, they needed to know about it sooner than later. He was going to make sure she knew how stupid she was being by not calling Lugow as soon as it happened. Did she want them to catch this guy or not?

CHAPTER ELEVEN

Eric parked the truck and headed into the hotel attached to the address. He knew he was looking for a party of sorts. He found a sign pointing him to an awards dinner and texted Donna's phone.

Where are you?

Grand Ballroom, first floor.

Awards dinner?

Yep.

On my way.

Eric made his way through the casino to the Grand Ballroom where he flashed his badge to gain access to the party. He walked into the large room. He scanned the crowd for any sign of Donna or Rebecca. He spotted Donna at a table just outside the bar area and she waved him over.

"Hey, thanks for coming."

"Thanks for the address."

"What's going on?'

"I think she got a visit from our friend this evening," he replied, still looking for Rebecca.

"Really, when?"

"Not sure, that's what I'm here to find out. Where is she?"

"Other side of the bar," Donna replied with a small wince.

His eyes found her. She was sitting on top of the bar, laughing and teasing a group of men surrounding her.

"She started doing shots, as soon as she hung up on you."

"Okay," he replied with a deep breath and wondered how he was going to handle this. She looked like she was having fun, although his stomach clenched at the thought of someone else's arms around her. "Maybe I should just leave her be. She's been through enough the past few days."

"Which is exactly why you need to go over there," Donna insisted. "She's not thinking straight. She isn't listening to me and Charlie isn't available."

The comment wasn't meant to, but it stung. He was third on the list. Fourth, if you counted Mindy. Eric nodded in agreement and walked around the bar to the engaging crowd. Perched on the bar, her long legs were crossed and wrapped in a mid-length black skirt. She wasn't flaunting anything, she was just smiling and laughing. The small gathering of men were making comments and even began singing to her.

Eric stood at the back of the group, waiting for her to see him. He couldn't help but become lost in the sight of her. Since their unexpected reunion, he hadn't really been able to just look at her, take her in and see once again how stunning she was. From her fiery locks to her thin ankles. His entire body began to pulse at the memory of her softness beneath him. He took a deep breath as her eyes caught his and instead of the expected scowl, she smiled and tilted her head as she had in the coffee shop.

"Look out, boys, the cops are here to rescue me," she said as she leaned forward.

He pushed his way between her suitors until his chest brushed against her legs. "May I have this dance?" he asked as he looked up into her eyes.

"Depends," she answered as her hands rested on his shoulders.

Eric grasped her waist and lifted her off the bar, resting her on the floor in front of him. "On what?"

"Whether you're here for business or pleasure."

"Dancing with you," he said in a low breath, as his body

reacted to her softness against him, his hands still wrapped around her small waist. "Definitely pleasure."

She looked up at him and the room seemed to disappear. A serenity that he'd only felt once before encompassed him. The weight of the world seemed to lift when he stared into the electric pools of her eyes, and he wondered how that could be.

"I wish that were true," she said.

He saw doubt and pain flash in her eyes. "Rebecca . . ." he started when the popping of a champagne bottle startled her. She jumped away from him as her entire body visibly trembled. She ran her fingers through her hair, and he watched her look for something familiar. Her eyes found Donna and she walked past him to her friend.

"What's he doing here?"

"I asked him to come. What happened at the house, Beccs?"

"Nothing, why?"

"Rebecca, I saw the flowers," Eric cut in, his voice low and discreet.

"You don't know what you're talking about," she objected in fury to Eric. "You're not supposed to be here!"

"Beccs, calm down, it's okay," Donna tried to reassure her.

Eric watched her body tense and tremble uncontrolled.

"No it's not all right, Don," she replied in desperation. "I'm . . . this is ruining your night! This is your night, Don."

"No, Beccs, it's fine! You aren't ruining anything!"

"I have to go," Rebecca replied as she moved past Donna into the crowd.

Eric and Donna both followed her through the crowd. They arrived back at the table just as Rebecca found her purse. She stepped to Donna, who pulled her into a hug before she moved to leave. Eric watched her turn to leave when her face drained of color. Her knees buckled and she began to collapse.

"Beccs," Donna called.

He reached out to break her fall. Eric managed to pull her alongside him as she went down. Bending his knees, he eased her descent and she fell limp into his arms.

"I'll get some water," Donna said.

Eric was left cradling her in his arms. "Rebecca," he said, calling to her as he smoothed the hair off her cheek. His own heart was pounding uncontrollably and he felt helpless as he looked at her pale closed eyes. "Beccs, can you hear me?"

Her eyes started to flutter and he brushed her cheek with his thumb, trying to coax her back to him.

"Beccs, can you hear me?" he said again, hoping his voice would allow her to focus. "Open your eyes, Beccs. If you can hear me, I need you to open your eyes."

"Eric?"

His chest swelled, realizing it was the first time she'd ever said his name. A peeking of blue showed beneath her heavy lids before they revealed themselves and his heart leapt in relief.

"Hey, bright eyes," he said, unable to subdue the smile that spread across his face. "Welcome back."

"Beccs," Donna said as she knelt beside them and handed him a bottled water. "Are you okay?"

"She's gonna be just fine," Eric said as he lifted her with his arm so she could take a drink of water. It was then he realized the audience surrounding them and he wondered how long they'd been watching. The color began to return to her cheeks and his breathing eased a little more. Rebecca took another sip and then Donna took the water as she glanced to Eric. "You think you can get up?"

Rebecca nodded and he helped her to her feet his arms still around her. She stood on her own for a moment, but her legs decided they didn't want to cooperate. Eric held her against him, not allowing her to fall. He moved her into one of the chairs next to the table. Lowering himself in front of her, she still seemed a little fuzzy and disoriented.

"We need to get her out of here," Eric commented as he rose to his feet, looking to Donna. "Did you guys bring separate cars?"

"No, Beccs drove," Donna replied.

This seemed to get Rebecca's attention as she looked at him in confusion.

"Do you know where her car is?"

"Yeah."

"Why don't you go get it and meet us out front," Eric suggested as Donna grabbed Rebecca's keys and disappeared.

"Where did Donna go?" she asked in a sweet weakened voice.

He pulled up a chair beside her. "To get your car."

"I'm sorry."

"There is nothing to be sorry for," he said, his heart aching as her eyes began to tear and he leaned forward, brushing a rebel tear off her cheek. "Are you ready to get out of here?"

She nodded as she rose from the chair, her limbs still shaking. His arm wrapped around her as he led the way out of the ballroom. Within a few minutes, they stepped into the hallway that led to the casino. He stayed beside her and they eventually made it through the main doors where Donna was waiting for them.

"Pull to the end of the valet lot. I'll meet you over there and follow you home," Eric said to Donna as Rebecca put on her seatbelt and he laid her phone in her lap.

"Perfect," Donna replied with a nod as Rebecca looked at Donna.

Eric caught sight of something on the ground at her feet. Reaching down, he lifted the single rose into the light. "See you in a bit," he said as he closed the door.

She just wanted to sleep. She wanted to close her eyes and fall into peaceful darkness for years. She remained quiet on the way to Donna's. She thought of the sleepless night ahead and almost wanted to cry.

They arrived at the apartment and got out of the car. Donna led them up the stairs and Rebecca leaned on the railing of the second floor porch. Donna unlocked the door and Eric joined them.

Why can't I just have an ordinary night? Just once?

She then scolded herself for complaining, it could be worse.

Much worse.

Eric entered the apartment first and they followed. Rebecca laid down her purse as the door closed, the sound making her jump and tremble. She walked out of the living room, irritated with herself, to get water from the fridge.

She flipped on the light and looked at the fridge. Instead, she came face to face with a blood-dripping mutilated canine corpse. Her lungs froze as she tried to step back. She heard a scream from outside herself. The next conscious thought was when she found herself cocooned within a strong chest and protective arms. It blanketed her from the sight as she tried to breathe.

This isn't happening.

"Rebecca."

She heard someone call to her, but couldn't get her body to respond to her commands. All she could do was cling to the arms around her until the world ceased to spin. Her entire body trembled uncontrolled as she tried to open her eyes. She looked up and saw him nodding to someone.

She felt her knees weaken beneath her and grabbed onto him for support. She saw him look down at her just as the room began to gray. She felt herself lifted and gripped his neck. She rested her head on his shoulder.

She heard voices, but couldn't make out what they were saying. She was so tired and felt safe in his arms. She let herself sink into the darkness, unwilling to relinquish the safe warm feeling that had embraced her.

She opened her eyes and saw the room bathed with a warm sunlight. She felt awake and refreshed like she'd just woken from a revitalizing sleep. Pushing the covers away and taking a deep breath, she got out of bed, walked to the door of her bedroom and opened it. It was dark and cold. The ground beneath her was wet and rough.

Looking around she was in the parking lot outside the rehab facility. She heard the revving of an engine and turning, the headlights of a large truck blinded her. Covering her eyes with her arms, she recognized the truck as Eric's and called his name, but nothing came out of her mouth. The truck revved again and jumped forward at her. She fell, landing hard on her back and when she opened her eyes, was in the hospital.

Sitting up she found herself in the middle of the hallway. Getting to her feet, she could hear screaming behind her. She ran toward it, down the hall, as it opened into a larger room. Her feet slid on the floor as she moved. Looking down, she saw red all around her, the screaming started again and she ran toward it.

Rebecca.

Hearing the voice echoing in the room, she turned, coming face to face with Charlie, Donna and Mindy all hanging from the wall, their throats slit. She screamed, but nothing came out.

Rebecca.

Turning again, she saw a layer of plastic in the corner of the room.

Rebecca.

It called to her, pulling her forward. Reaching out, she pushed the plastic away, seeing Eric and Lucy both tied to chairs and bleeding. Rebecca ran toward them when she was stopped, feeling someone behind her.

Rebecca.

Rebecca turned, knowing the sound of the voice and saw her mother standing behind her, wearing a bloodied white nightgown and holding a knife . . .

Mom?

Choose, Rebecca . . .

Rebecca looked back to Eric and Lucy sitting in their chairs and then back to her mother. She'd disappeared. Rebecca turned back to Eric and Lucy, seeing her mother standing between the two a gun in each hand pointed at their heads.

Too late.

Rebecca bolted up feeling a hand on her chest, hearing herself screaming. Opening her eyes, she saw nothing but blackness. She pushed away whatever was touching her.

"Beccs, stop, you're safe."

She turned.

Donna was staring back at her in fear and concern.

Blinking Rebecca forced herself to take a breath and sit back in the bed.

"Are you okay?"

"Yeah," she replied, still breathless as the images continued to run on a loop in her mind. "It was just a bad dream."

"Are you sure?"

"Yeah, I'm good," she replied with a nod and a smile as she ran her fingers through her hair. She remembered the skinned dog and trembled again. She felt Donna lay down in the bed beside her and turned to look at her. "I lost it, didn't I?"

"It happens," Donna replied with a small shrug. "I was right there with you except I ran for the bathroom."

"Eri . . . Detective Stiles was here, wasn't he?"

"Yeah he was . . . do you remember what happened?"

"I remember the dog, after that . . . it's blank," she admitted. "How horribly did I embarrass myself? Oh my God and it was twice in one night!"

"Stop it, you're being ridiculous," Donna replied with a sigh. "You're lucky you've made it as far as you have, sweetheart. The mind and the body can only take so much."

"I suppose," she replied, her mind settling on Eric's eyes as they looked down at her, his arms as they held her.

God . . . she was losing it . . .

"You should try and go back to sleep," Donna suggested, breaking through her daydream.

"Will you stay with me?" she asked, her stomach clenching at the thought of being alone.

"Of course," Donna replied as she took her hand and squeezed.

Rebecca held onto her friend's warm hand, it was small but a source of comfort. She felt she could breathe and even drift.

For a little while at least . . .

Chapter Twelve

Rebecca unlocked the door of her house. It was just after 5 AM and her head was swimming. Trudging into the bathroom, she turned on the shower and stripped off the sweats and t-shirt Donna had loaned her. She stepped beneath the hot streams of water as she tried not to think about the previous evening. She tried not to think about him and the way her entire body melted when he touched her.

I wish that were true.

What was that? She was such an idiot, what was he going to say in response?

She allowed the alcohol and nerves to take over, which landed her on the floor. Somehow, her rational levelheaded self disappeared and she literally tripped over herself. The thought of it was mortifying, but she had to admit seeing his smiling face when she opened her eyes wasn't that horrible.

Then it got so much worse. Her body betrayed her and he had to practically carry her to the car. Where he found the rose, of course, and then returned her cell phone as if rubbing her lack of control in her face.

The man is infuriating!

She leaned her head against the cool tile and part of her wished he'd just leave her alone. Her entire body ached as she allowed herself to imagine never seeing him again. She was so tired of having this same argument with herself. She pushed the internal conversation from her mind as she got out of the shower.

The bed looked so inviting, but she knew it would be

pointless. She dressed, started a pot of coffee and booted up her laptop to do some much-needed work. An hour later she realized her attempt to concentrate was in vain. She poured herself another cup of coffee and sipped it.

After waking from her nightmare, she'd spent the remainder of the night watching movies on Donna's couch. She'd dozed off twice, but awakened again with screaming nightmares.

Leaning across the counter, she stared down into the steaming cup of caffeine, wanting to just sleep. She took another sip as her head began to throb.

There was a knock at the door.

Rebecca looked at it in alarm. She considered acting like she wasn't home. She moved to the door. She looked through the peephole to see Eric. Taking a deep breath, she opened the door.

"Detective . . ." she greeted as he looked back at her. His eyes were apprehensive and urgent as she reminded herself that he was off limits. In the world they lived in, Dallas never happened.

"Where's Donna?" he asked, moving past her into the house.

"I would assume at home, why?"

"Mindy?"

"Home, I guess, I don't know . . ."

"Exactly my point, what the hell are you doing?"

"What . . ."

"It's not okay for you to be by yourself, Rebecca. Someone out there is trying to hurt you."

"I'm not having this conversation with you," she replied in shock and annoyance at his scolding.

"Yes we are having this conversation," he replied as he took a step closer to her.

She saw the fear in his eyes.

"You need to start being more careful, this isn't a game."

"What exactly have I done to make you think that this is a game to me?" she asked, her temper and emotions fraying from lack of sleep.

"You're going to get yourself killed."

"So I'm just supposed to hide until it goes away? I'm supposed to stop my entire life while I wait for someone to catch him?"

"No, but you need to stop taking unnecessary risks."

"Okay, hang on a sec, let's just review what risks I'm allowed to take," she replied, the sarcasm dripping from her voice. "So we've established I'm not safe at home, since I've spent almost two weeks with Donna now. So according to you, home is out."

"Beccs . . ."

"So what about work? Nope, can't do that either, parade of flowers, a rotting teddy bear and a box of blood pretty much shut that door, didn't it?"

"You're not hearing me . . ."

"No, Eric, you're not hearing me. I can't go to work, I can't come home, what else is there?"

"You need to think about this for a minute."

"No I don't! I'm tired of thinking about it," she snapped as her voice cracked and her eyes started to tear. "That's all I do is think about it! I lay awake at night seeing flowers, boxes of blood and dead rats. Not to mention hear the screams of unknown women as they have God knows what done to them!"

"Beccs, calm down," he said as he reached out to touch her.

She backed away, the sound of pounding in her head. "I'm done thinking about it. I'm done running from this asshole," she snapped, unable to keep the emotion out of her voice as she pushed her hand through her hair. "If he wants me, he can come and get me! In fact I hope he doesn't wait too long because I need to get some goddamn sleep!" Rebecca finished her rant and walked past him toward the door. Her intention was to open it in an effort to show him out.

"Rebecca . . ." he called in frustration.

She reached for the door.

There was a loud popping and the sound of breaking glass.

The noise barely registered before there were arms around her, pushing her to the floor. The popping sound continued and she covered her head with her arms, feeling him on top of her. The barrage seemed to stop and he shifted. His arms remained around her and she felt the warmth of his touch on her cheek as she opened her eyes.

"Are you okay?" he asked, his eyes soft and genuine as they looked at her.

"I think so," she whispered. She watched him rise off the floor beside her and then reach out his hand to help her to her feet. Her legs shook in protest beneath her. He pulled out his out his phone and the thickness of his steady hand rested on the small of her back. Rebecca looked into her living room. The floor was covered in shattered glass from the bay window.

"This is Detective Stiles, badge G28904. I need CSU and back up at 1435 Sahara Drive," he said into the phone.

She stepped back, using the wall for support. The world was spinning and she reminded herself to breathe as her sight began to gray.

"You should probably sit down."

"I'm fine," she refused as she straightened her posture in defiance. "What happened?"

"I don't know," he admitted as he edged toward the window, trying to examine it.

Her hands trembled as she pushed them through her hair.

"So what happens now?" she asked as she moved to the kitchen, desperate to hide her uncontrolled physical reaction to the event.

"What do you mean?"

She made herself busy at the coffeepot. "You just called the station. It's not a stretch to assume that my house is about to be flooded with uniforms," she replied, willing herself back under control.

"Yes."

"And you were here during the whole . . . thing."

"I . . ."

"You don't really need me," she commented as she turned toward him. She thought he was across the room, but was instead standing just few feet away. "You're the expert so you can tell them . . ."

"Rebecca, you're not leaving."

"There is no reason for me to stay," she rationalized as she turned away from him, wiping her palms on her jeans. "You and your police buddies have plenty to do and I'll just get in the way."

"You're not in the way."

"You were here so they won't need my statement. You can take care of all . . ." she continued as she leaned against the counter, staring down at the floor.

"Rebecca," he said.

She remembered the feel of his strong hands holding her close. She tried to breathe as she watched him approach her from across the kitchen. "And to be honest I would really rather not be here as you go through my life looking for evidence," she continued to protest as her insides knotted. He came within a few inches of her and she fought for control.

"Rebecca, look at me," he said in a calm soothing tone that she resented as his hands wrapped around her arms. "Breathe."

She couldn't help but obey and hence became trapped in his gaze. His eyes were just as she remembered them, expressive and deep. His hand grazed her hair and she was taken back to Dallas, the familiar warmth of him enveloping her. She hadn't realized that her eyes closed, but when they opened, he was just inches away.

His hand brushed against her hair. Her eyes closed with his touch and his breath caught in his throat. No matter how much he'd convinced himself that he hadn't wanted to touch her again, there was no way to deny it now. Her gleaming eyes looked up at him and he could see the fire behind the cool blue. The flames called to him and he fell into them without hesitation.

A shrilling ring echoed through the house, and he felt her lurch beneath his hands, breaking the spell.

She shifted away from him as she walked to the phone.

He forced himself to exhale and bury the ignited heat that had encapsulated him.

"Hello," she said into the phone.

He scratched the back of his head and turned to face her.

"Who is this?"

He didn't think she could get any paler, but saw he was wrong. He moved without hesitation toward her as she pulled the phone away from her ear. She pushed the speaker and record button on the phone so he could hear. As it clicked over, they heard the sound of garbled laughing.

"I can't wait to hear you scream, Rebecca," a deep threatening voice said before they heard the sound of a woman's scream bellow from the phone. Eric dialed his cell as Rebecca backed away from the phone. The woman continued to wail and then began to scream Rebecca's name. Eric watched her cringe as the unknown woman pleaded for Rebecca to make it stop. The call lasted for another ten seconds and then there was a dial tone.

His gaze still on her, Eric hung up the phone. A flash of fear and vulnerability echoed her eyes, begging him for comfort. They both heard a knock and the helplessness in her face disappeared. It was replaced by the steel cool strength he'd come to know.

She moved to the door, inviting the stream of blue jackets into her house.

Lug arrived with them and took Rebecca into the next room to get her statement. The teams began to work the scene as Eric sent the recording of the phone call to the tech unit. After her interview was complete, she kept her distance. He found her in the corner of the kitchen, watching, her arms crossed against her chest.

They found six separate charges on the outside of her windows with only enough explosive to do damage to the window. The timed triggers were set to go off after Rebecca left her house.

So why go through all the trouble to terrorize her?

What did this guy or these people want from her?

Eric heard a phone ring and he turned as she answered it. Her living room was in pieces all over the floor and he'd just finished scolding her for not taking the situation seriously.

Brilliant Stiles . . .

From the corner of his eye, he saw her grabbing her purse and heading for the door. "Rebecca," he called as she left the house. "Rebecca, stop!"

She continued to walk.

He ran to catch her. She reached the edge of the lawn when he got close enough to touch her arm. He turned her to face him. "Beccs, stop." She faced him with enraged eyes and he forgot what he was going to say.

"Let go!"

"Where are you going?"

"None of your business," she replied as she pulled out of his grasp.

"Rebecca . . ." he called to her again as she got in her car and sped off.

"Where the hell is she going?" Lug asked as he joined him on the lawn.

"I don't know."

"You going after her?"

"Yeah," Eric said as he moved to his truck.

"Call me when you get there."

Chapter Thirteen

Two hours later, she pulled into the parking lot. With little memory of how she'd gotten there, she ran into the hospital, stopping at the nurse's desk. "My name is Rebecca Gailen, I'm here to see Dr. Schaffer about my sister," she said.

"I'll check the register if you want to just take a seat."

"No, I don't think you understand," Rebecca replied. "Dr. Schaffer called me to come down here as soon as possible. I need to see him now."

"Miss, there are over sixty patients in this facility handled by Dr. Schaffer, now if you will just take a seat," the nurse insisted, her face pinched in irritation.

"There's something wrong with my sister. Please, if you could just page him, he's expecting me."

"It's not policy . . ."

"Fuck your policy!" Rebecca cursed at the woman before she moved past the desk and through the doors marked *Staff Only*.

"Rebecca!" a male voice called accompanied by running footsteps.

Turning, she saw Dr. Schaffer as he jogged to meet her. "Where's Lucy?"

"She's okay."

"I want to see her."

"I'll take you to her," he replied as he rested his hand on her arm, ushering her down a long hallway through a second set of double doors. He escorted her into an observation room where, via a pane of glass, she saw Lucy lying unconscious in a hospital bed hooked to various IV lines and monitors

"What happened?" Rebecca asked as she stared at her sister, trying to keep her emotions at bay.

"She and another patient knocked the guard and two of the nurses unconscious before stealing meds from the drug closet. They both overdosed. Lucy was lucky that we found her before . . . the other patient wasn't as fortunate."

"Whose idea was it?"

"We're not sure, we're still interviewing the other patients to get the details."

"I thought you said she was doing better?"

"Rebecca, the reason Lucy started using heroine was in an attempt to self-medicate," he started to explain. "I've been able to diagnose and we've started her on medication, but it's going to take some time."

"She's manic, isn't she?"

"Yes."

"Is it as bad as Mom's?"

"We don't know yet, but things are different now. The disease is manageable. She can live a normal life."

"Does she know?"

"Yes, I told her a few days ago."

"Why didn't you call me?"

"She didn't want you here."

"You knew what she'd do! You know how much she hated . . ." Rebecca scolded him in frustration. "I should have been here! You should have called me!"

"I'm Lucy's doctor, Rebecca. I have to abide by her wishes. There was nothing you could've done," he defended. "She needs to deal with this alone. Come to terms with it in her own time."

"Alone," Rebecca started, staring at her sister's motionless form behind the glass. "That worked well."

"You have to understand—"

"When can I talk to her?"

"She doesn't—"

"I need to talk to my sister, Dr. Shaffer."

"She's been sedated and should come around in about an hour or so."

"Can I sit with her until then?"

"Unfortunately not, this ward is in lockdown," he replied.

She clenched her fists in frustration.

"But if you'd like to sit in here and wait, you're welcome to."

"Thank you," she said as she continued to stare beyond the glass, wondering if Lucy was in any kind of pain.

"Rebecca," Dr Shaffer called.

She moved to face him.

"Believe it or not, this is a good thing. She's hit rock bottom, there's nowhere to go but up from here."

She heard the door close and it was everything she could do not to fall apart. Her very worst fears were staring her in the face, and she was powerless to do anything. Lucy had inherited their mother's disease. It had always been a possibility, but Rebecca had thought they'd gotten clear of the threat.

Images of her mother's fits of screaming tantrums followed by days and nights of motionless silence pounded at her mind. She fought against the fear the diagnosis brought. There were new therapies, drugs that could balance the chemicals and allow her sister to live a normal life.

Rebecca looked for her phone to call Donna and realized she'd left it in the car. Deciding she needed air anyway, a few minutes later, she pushed through the main doors of the facility and was blinded with the bright sunlight. She closed her eyes against the warmth. She folded her arms against her chest as she made her way across the parking lot.

She looked at her car and stopped when she saw him leaning against it, waiting for her. Her steps quickened in fury and she was within a few feet. "What the hell are you doing here?" she asked as she opened the car door and pulled out her cell phone.

"Wondering where we are."

"We aren't anywhere," she replied as she slammed the door before facing Eric in fury. "And you're leaving!"

"No I don't think I am," he replied, his eyes boring through her. "Given the redness around your eyes I would say you could use a friend about now."

"And yet there you stand, Detective Stiles," she snapped as she turned to leave.

"Rebecca, wait," he pleaded.

She stopped, but kept her back to him.

"I don't know what's going on . . ."

"What part of *it's none of your business* do you not understand?" she asked as she turned. "What are you doing here? You followed me?"

"No, I just . . . yes I followed you. You shouldn't be alone right now. It's not safe. "

"Well I'm releasing you from your obligation, Detective. I'm fine, so you and your badge can go help someone else."

"Beccs," he called.

She stopped again, feeling her defenses against him weakening.

"I'm not here as a badge."

"Don't . . ." she started as she turned, wanting to scold him for being such an ass.

"There's no badge, I'm here as a friend only," he said as he walked to meet her, his eyes pleading. "I'm not going to just leave you here alone. Not like this."

She decided not to reply to his statement, but instead, relented to his request by walking back to her car and leaning against the trunk.

"So what is this place?" he asked as he moved to meet her.

She studied his gentle eyes and wavy brown hair. "It's the Xavier Center for Rehabilitation."

"Drug Rehabilitation?"

"Yeah."

"Who's here, Beccs?"

"My sister," Rebecca nodded and wished for her sunglasses to hide her eyes from him. Going back to her car, she reached inside and grabbed them off the dash. She hadn't wanted him to know she'd been crying and wanted to be able to hide it if she started again.

"So I'm going to assume by the way you tore out of your driveway that this isn't a regular visit?"

Rebecca put on her sunglasses and leaned against the trunk again, staring at the hospital. *Maybe if I'd come sooner, when she wanted to see me, this wouldn't have happened. I should've known that there was something wrong when she fell off the grid. I waited too long to go looking for her. If I'd gotten to her sooner . . .*

"Beccs?"

She debated her answer for a moment. "She overdosed," Rebecca replied as she dipped her head, staring down at the blacktop beneath her feet.

"Is she okay?"

"For now," she answered with a nod before she looked back at the hospital. "She's sedated and I won't be able to see her for a while, but the doctor says she's going to be okay."

"What can I do?"

"I'm hungry," she offered, feeling sorry for him. He was just trying to help and she was glad to have someone to keep her company.

"Okay, so if we have some time, why don't you let me

take you to get something to eat?"

She nodded which brought a smile to his lips. "I just need to let them know."

"I'll grab the truck and meet you at the door."

Eric jogged to his truck and pulled it around, waiting for her to appear from inside the hospital. He wasn't sure what he was doing, but it felt right and she wasn't fighting him so he was going to go with it.

A few moments later, she was getting into the truck and they were on the road. They drove for a few miles and found a small roadside diner. Eric pulled in. "Does this look okay?"

She nodded as she pulled on the door handle and got out.

He got out as well, following her up the steps and pulled open the main door as she walked through. A trucker favorite by the signs and hats that littered the edges of the room, a polite older waitress led them to a booth beside a window and asked what they'd like to drink.

"Coffee, please," Rebecca said as she pulled off her sunglasses, looking to him.

"Make it two, please," he added as his eyes met hers. The feeling was familiar and the calm he remembered from that night began to wash over him despite the circumstances. He watched her look over the menu, wanting to know what to say to her. Wanting to know what to do. He had nothing, so he just sat there, feeling useless again.

The waitress reappeared beside their table, putting two cups of coffee and a tin of cream in front of them with a smile.

"Have you decided what you'd like, darlins?"

"I'll have a grilled sticky bun please," Rebecca said as she closed the menu, looking at him.

"SOS with a side of bacon, please," Eric requested as he

watched the waitress write something on her pad, take their menus and disappear. "Someone has a sweet tooth."

"Not usually, but today is an exception to the rule," she replied as she poured cream into her coffee.

"So that was the phone call you got at the house?"

"Yes. They called and said I needed to get to the hospital as soon as possible," she replied, pouring sugar in her coffee and stirring it with her spoon. "It wasn't until I got there that I found out the story."

"What happened?" he asked, watching for her reaction.

She looked up and then picked up her coffee, taking a sip. "Lucy made a friend and they broke into the medicine closet. She took a bottle of something and they found her and her friend. They were able to save Lucy, but not her friend."

"Beccs, I'm so sorry," he said in shock. "Were you able to see her at all?"

"They put me in an observation room, she's hooked up to an IV and a few monitors, but the doctor said she'll be okay."

"Do they have any idea why she . . ."

"Not for sure, but I have an idea," she replied hesitantly as she looked at him.

It was as if she were searching for something in his eyes. Some kind of confirmation and he met her gaze, trying to confirm whatever it was she was looking for. *You can trust me, please talk to me.*

The look was broken as the little waitress arrived with their food.

Eric dropped the subject, wanting her to eat. They each took a few bites and then he heard Rebecca place her fork on her plate. He looked up at her in concern and she put her hand in her hair, leaning her elbow on the table.

"My mother killed herself when I was nineteen," she said, her eyes steady with his. "She was manic depressive and one day she decided she couldn't deal with it anymore. Six months later, I became Lucy's legal guardian."

"What about your dad?"

"He left when I was twelve. He couldn't handle my mother's instability," she explained as she sat back, raising her coffee cup to her lips. "The doctor said that Lucy was using heroine to self-medicate. He's diagnosed her manic as well."

The calmness that she displayed as she talked about it stunned him, but he guessed she'd been dealing with the reality for a long time.

"I'm pretty sure that's where this is stemming from."

"It's good that they diagnosed it. Now they can treat it and she can move on with her life," he said.

She nodded before returning to her food.

The conversation ended and they finished their food as Eric tried to wrap his mind around what she was going through. The news, while upsetting, was a good thing, right? He didn't understand why, when she looked at him, he continued to see hopelessness.

Half an hour later, Eric paid the check and they headed back out to the truck in silence. He got in the driver's side and sat a moment, looking over at her staring out the window."Beccs," he started, getting her attention as she put her sunglasses back on. "You can't blame yourself for your sister's mistakes."

"It's not that easy."

"She messed up," he said as he turned toward her. "It happens to the best of us. You need to let her deal with it."

"You don't know what you're talking about so just drop it."

"So explain it to me," he replied as she got out of the truck and he followed her, meeting her at the back of the truck. "Tell me why this is your fault?"

"I never said —"

"You didn't say it wasn't," he replied as he watched her body tense. "Do you think there's something you could've done to prevent this? Did you somehow know this was going to happen?

"Of course not!"

"Then why are you beating yourself up about it?"

"I just . . . I should've known! I'm supposed to take care of her! I should've known that there was something wrong! I must've done something wrong somewhere along the way to cause this. Was her life not stable enough? Was I too hard on her, was I not hard enough?"

"Rebecca, I'm sure you did the best you could," he offered as he watched in agony as she beat herself up.

"My baby sister is lying in a rehab hospital bed sedated, because she tried to kill herself. Whatever I did, it wasn't good enough, Eric!"

"None of this is your fault," he said, grasping her hand in reassurance as he moved closer to her. "*What ifs* and *should haves* will drive you crazy. It is what it is and you can handle it."

He could tell she was avoiding his gaze even with the sunglasses, and he tugged on her hand to get her to face him. Eric reached out and pulled the sunglasses from her eyes, seeing them brimming with tears. He tucked her hair behind her ear as she tried to smile at him, but it came out as a shuddered breath.

He couldn't take it anymore. He pulled her into his chest and wrapped his arms around her in a hug. She hugged him back and his heart surged without restraint. Eric couldn't help but close his eyes as he savored her against him.

They heard the beeping of a horn behind them and they broke their embrace to walk around to the side of the truck. He looked at her with a sigh and she wiped away her tears with back of her hand before squeezing his hand.

"I'd better get back to the hospital," she said.

He nodded in agreement, releasing her hand with a tugging regret. They both climbed into the truck and arrived back at the hospital. Eric pulled up alongside the doors, looking at her. "Hey, you okay?"

"Yeah," she said hesitantly. "I want you to meet Lucy."

"Uh . . . okay, are you sure?" he asked in confusion and she nodded. "I'll meet you inside?"

"No, actually can you park the truck? There's something I need to tell you before we go inside," she said as her hands twisted within themselves.

He parked his truck beside her car, turned off the engine and looked at her in curiosity. "So what's going on?"

"You have to understand that I didn't tell you to protect her."

"Who?"

"Lucy."

"Okay back up, what didn't you tell me exactly?" he asked.

She stared at him. "I kidnapped her," she started.

He became even more confused.

"Or rather I rescued her."

"What?"

"About five months ago I received a return of Lucy's tuition check from Seattle College. They told me she'd dropped out. I waited a few weeks for her to call before I went looking for her. She never called and for lack of a better word, she vanished.

"Two months ago I flew to Seattle to find her. I managed to track down some of her college friends and got the basic story of why she'd dropped out. She met a guy. Things got serious pretty fast and she moved in with him. Once that happened, the only time anyone who knew her would ever see her was at a party or bar. Then they stopped seeing her at all.

"I got a name, I did my homework and I followed him home one night. I waited until I knew for sure she was with him and then . . . I waited for him to leave the house and went in to talk to her. I found her high and half-dead. I grabbed her and took her out to the car. She was so weak she didn't even try to resist."

"It sounds like it was a good thing you got her out of there, Beccs."

"Eric, when we were leaving, her . . . her boyfriend came back."

"What happened?"

"Once I got her in the car, Lucy asked me to go back for something. He caught me as I was leaving. I managed to get away from him, but as I pulled away, he shot at the car. He blew out the back windshield, but we managed to get far enough away before he could fire again."

"Beccs . . ." Eric started, his mind attempting to process what she was telling him.

"I know, I should have told you sooner, I'm sorry," she said in honest regret as he met her eyes.

"It's okay," he replied with a nod, knowing that this wasn't the time or place to request further details. "We'll talk about it later. Right now, you need to get in and see Lucy."

"Will you still come with me?"

"Of course," he said as they both got out of the truck.

They crossed the parking lot together and Eric stopped at the doors.

"What's up?"

"I forgot about the cellular policy and I need to check in with my partner. Go ahead, I'll be just a minute."

"Okay."

"Beccs?"

"Yeah?"

"What was Lucy's boyfriend's name?"

"Marco Valnes," she replied before she turned back and disappeared into the hospital.

Eric dialed Adam's number and relayed Rebecca's story. He finished and jogged into the hospital, seeing her waiting at the desk. The nurse asked him for ID and then a male nurse led them back into the belly of the facility.

He left them outside a set of closed rooms and as he walked away, Eric looked at Rebecca who was once again confident and strong. "Where are we exactly?"

"I'm not sure, this is different than where they brought me before," she replied as they heard approaching footsteps and then saw a doctor. Rebecca seemed to recognize him as he introduced himself to Eric.

"How is she?"

"Better, she's just waking up," he replied.

Eric took that as a good sign.

"You'll only be able to see her for a few minutes, Rebecca, she needs to rest. Too much too soon can have negative effects on her. I'll be watching from the observation room if you need anything."

"Would it be all right if Eric went with you?"

"That's fine," the doctor replied with a small nod as Rebecca looked at him and then turned toward the door of Lucy's room.

Eric followed the doctor into an observation room, not that unlike the ones they used at the station. Rebecca walked into the adjacent room and Eric watched as she sat down on the edge of the bed, taking Lucy's hand.

Sound filled the small room and they could hear the conversation.

"Hey, sweetie, how are you feeling?"

"What do you want?"

"I wanted to make sure you're okay."

"I'm the same as when you left me here."

"Lucy, I know it's hard, but we're gonna get through this."

"We? There is no we, Beccs. You and your perfect fucking life. There is no we! You dumped me here and forgot about me."

"That's not true," Rebecca said in a broken voice.

Eric looked at the doctor who stood calmly watching.

"Yes it is! You abandoned me just like you abandoned Mom. It was your fault!"

"Lucy . . ."

"She killed herself because of you! She couldn't get you to stay out of her life and now you're doing it to me!" Lucy screamed.

Eric saw the flash of metal in Lucy's raised hand. He was the first one out the door with the doctor behind him. The door opened and Eric saw Lucy screaming. She straddled Rebecca on the floor, threatening her with a hypodermic needle.

"*Lucy stop!*" the doctor called as Rebecca was in a dead lock with Lucy, the hypodermic in the balance. Two orderlies arrived and Eric heard the doctor tell them to freeze as there was no way for them to get to the women.

"Beccs, talk to her," Eric called to her, his police training kicking in.

"Lucy, think about what you're doing, sweetie. You don't want to hurt me."

"*Shut up!*"

"Okay, Lucy, fine. If this is what you want then, I'm going to let go and you do what you need to do."

"*I hate you!*"

"You hate me? Fine, end it now. I'll be out of your life forever and you'll be alone just like you want," Rebecca shot back at her with a strong mothering tone as she released her hand off Lucy's.

Eric watched as Lucy's hand fell and Rebecca used it as leverage to throw her off balance. She rolled the girl onto her back, in turn, pinning her to the ground. Lucy screamed bloody murder, but Rebecca stayed strong.

"I hate you! You fucking whore, I hate you! I hate you!"

The doctor stepped forward, sedative in hand. He injected Lucy and Rebecca held her for another moment before she drifted off. As soon as she relaxed, Rebecca and the orderlies lifted her onto the bed. She covered her with the blankets before she smoothed the hair off her face.

"Rebecca," the doctor called

Eric turned, following him out of the room.

Rebecca kissed her sister's forehead and followed.

"Are you all right?"

"I'm fine, have you started treatment for the MD yet?"

"No, Lucy . . ."

"I have power of attorney and, as she's currently incapacitated, I want you to begin treatment of her," she said to the doctor who nodded. "I'll need a full S.O.W. including all meds, emailed to me in the next twenty-four hours."

"Rebecca, are you sure this is what you want to do? Lucy doesn't . . ."

"Lucy can make decisions when she's lucid enough to do so, until then, this is what she needs."

"Okay. I'll just need you to sign some paperwork and I'll get to work." The doctor disappeared down the hall.

Rebecca turned, facing him. Eric met her eyes and he could see her holding back the dam of emotions that threatened to pour out. He grasped her hand and she took a deep breath as they waited.

A few moments later, the doctor returned.

She read and signed a stack of forms, asked for copies and

they headed out of the hospital.

"You did good, Beccs," he said, trying to ease her worry as they reached his truck and she faced him. After a moment, she lowered her shoulders, looking up at him with a sigh and he noticed a blood stain on her shirt. Lifting her chin and examining her, he saw a long slice on the side of her neck.

"Jesus, Beccs, you're bleeding," he said as he tugged on her hand, leading her to the passenger side of his truck. He opened the door and pulled out the first aid kit from beneath the seat. He watched her search for the cut with her fingertips. He ripped open a pack of gauze and handed it to her. "Here."

She wasn't sure where she was going with it and he took her by the arms, directing her to the passenger's seat of the truck. Sitting her on the truck step, he took the gauze from her, holding it against the wound. "How did you not feel that?"

"Adrenaline?"

"Good answer," he replied with a small laugh as he switched hands, applying a fresh piece of gauze to her neck. "Hold that."

She raised her hand, holding the gauze as requested.

He pulled out the medical tape, tearing off a few strips. "You know, I should really take you back inside and have you checked out by a real doctor."

"It's a scratch."

"No, it's really not," Eric replied as he finished and brushed her hair over her shoulder. She stood, putting herself just inches from him. He leaned his arm against the truck as he smiled at her.

"Should I start calling you Dr. Stiles?" she asked as she rested against the truck, not removing herself from the space between his arm and the door.

"Possibly, but I think Field Medic . . ." he started and then heard her phone ring.

She reached into her pocket, pulling it out, and he saw Charlie's name.

He stepped back and she moved away as she took the call. Eric did his best not to listen to the conversation, trying to internalize his frustration with the situation yet again. He busied himself by putting away the first aid kit. He discarded the leftover supplies and shut the passenger side door. He walked around the back of the truck and saw her say goodbye to Charlie as she hung up the phone.

"We should probably head back," she said as she shoved her phone in her pocket and ran her fingers through her hair.

"Yeah," he said, unwilling to look at her again for fear that he'd burst.

"Home?"

"Home."

Chapter Fourteen

Rebecca pulled into the driveway and got out as Eric pulled up along the curb. He got out of the truck and walked around the front as she stared in disbelief at the front of her house.

"What's wrong?"

"My window's fixed."

"Yeah it is, why?"

"I didn't have time to call anyone and . . ." She turned to see a grin on his face. "You didn't . . ."

"You needed a new window and I had some time to kill when I was waiting outside the hospital."

"Eric, I can't believe you did this, how did you get around the alarm?"

"I'm a cop, I have connections."

"Good to know," she replied as she unlocked the door and stepped in, turning off the alarm as he walked in behind her. "At least let me give you money to cover the expense."

"Don't worry about it, a buddy of mine owed me a favor."

"Are you sure?"

"Positive," he replied as he closed the door behind them.

Rebecca laid her stuff on the kitchen counter and went to the fridge for something to drink. "Do you want a soda?"

"Sounds good," he replied.

She watched him looking over her house from the corner of her eye. She pulled out two sodas, put them on the counter and popped one of the tops. He heard her and moved toward the kitchen to join her.

"So do you rent this place?"

"Nope, I'm a proud owner, overpriced mortgage and all," she replied with a grin, still feeling fairly relaxed despite her breakdown with Lucy and the call from Charlie. It sounded cheesy, but something about Eric made her feel safe.

"Lucky you," he replied as he raised his can of soda to her.

"It's better than dumping rent money into someone else's pockets. It gives Lucy somewhere to come home to and it's small, but its mine."

"Hey, I think it's great. I wish I had the courage to do it," he replied with a grin.

His look made the heat rise in her neck. "So what's stopping you?"

"I don't know. I never really saw the need for anything permanent I guess. My dad lives in town and has a house, that's always been my anchor."

The doorbell rang.

She shrugged as she moved to it. Opening the door, she was greeted by three familiar smiling faces.

Mike, Donna and Mindy, who blew into the house like a whirlwind.

"What are you guys doing here?" she asked them as they all noticed Eric's presence.

"Dinner, remember?"

"Oh my God, I forgot," she said as she looked at the kitchen. "I have nothing to . . ."

"Do you like Chinese?" Eric asked the group.

"That's a great idea," Donna chimed in, catching Rebecca's eye. "There's that new place down on Jones."

"What? You guys haven't had Terry's take out?" Eric asked with a sideways grin.

"Terry's take out, never heard of it," Mike replied, shaking his head.

"Oh, you guys are missing out," Eric said as he pulled out his phone. "It's the best take out in town next to Dominic's."

Rebecca and Donna looked at him as he brought up the menu.

"Here, pick whatever you want, Terry is a friend of mine, I can get it cheap," Eric offered as he handed the phone to Mike and he started looking over the menu with Mindy.

"Is there anyone you don't know in this town?" Rebecca asked and he flashed that knee-melting smile at her again. She focused on his eyes as she walked toward him, yearning to just hug him. "So are you planning to stay for dinner?"

"If that was an invitation, yes," he replied.

She stopped about a foot away from him. He kept her gaze and she wondered what he was thinking. He reached out and tucked a stray curl behind her ear before he walked away. She watched him join Mindy and Mike who were writing down their orders.

Rebecca was frozen for an instant and then she turned, seeing Donna giving her the eye. She couldn't help but laugh and roll her eyes.

They got the order together and Rebecca went to give Eric money. He refused it as he headed out the door with Mike. As soon as the door closed, Donna and Mindy were on her like magnets to metal.

"What's he doing here?" Mindy asked, giddy with excitement.

Rebecca discreetly pulled the bandage off her neck and discarded it. Donna knew she'd been to see Lucy, but she wasn't in the mood to rehash all of the details again. "With Charlie gone, he stopped by to make sure I was okay," Rebecca replied, knowing it was a lie, but decided the whole truth was too long and complicated of a story.

"That was nice of him," Mindy commented as Donna remained silent.

Rebecca started stocking the freezer with beers for dinner.

"And you two were just chatting when we arrived?"

"Yes, Mindy, we were just chatting. Speaking of which, how are you doing?" Rebecca watched as Mindy shifted against the counter, unable to meet Rebecca's eyes.

"I'm fine, good," she replied with a half-smile.

Rebecca locked her eyes.

She relented. "Fine, I'm freaked out, okay?"

"You're supposed to be freaked out, Min," Donna offered as she gave her friend a sideways hug. "That's a normal reaction."

"I'm getting over it. Mike has been great. He stayed with me that first night and we've talked on the phone every night since."

"Sounds like you and Mike are getting close."

"We're just friends, right, Beccs?"

"What's that supposed to mean?"

"It means that you seem to be just friends with all sorts of people lately. We're all anxiously awaiting to see who is going to move into the more-than-friends category," Donna replied with a smirk, knowing full well she was putting Rebecca on the spot.

"So give us a hint, which one are you leaning toward? Charlie or Eric?"

"Mindy!"

"You know my opinion," Donna added with a wink.

"Come on, Beccs, I need leftovers."

"What about Mike?"

"Mike, Shmike, Charlie and or Eric are much juicier."

"Okay well if it's that important to you, why don't you tell me which one you don't want?"

"Hmmm, that is a tough choice," Mindy played along as she began to pace the small area of the kitchen. "Charlie is heroic, genuine and adorable. While Eric is dark, brooding and mysterious."

"Charlie is mysterious," Rebecca offered as she began pulling out glasses and plates. Donna and Mindy both turned looking at her and then she thought about what she'd said. "Okay maybe not so much . . . but he's honest and loyal. You know that he'd never cheat."

"Good point," Mindy agreed. "Eric is mysterious enough that he's either a diehard monogamist or a player."

"Why can't he be both?" Donna asked. "Maybe he just hasn't found the right girl yet. You know, that one that makes him want to settle down."

"Fairy tale," Mindy chided as Donna and Rebecca giggled. "We're dealing in reality, ladies. Let's stay focused, okay?"

"Yeah, because this whole conversation is so realistic."

"Regardless, a choice must be made," Mindy said as she and Donna both looked at Rebecca, putting her on the spot again. "You can't have them both."

"So choose already," Rebecca replied with a grin, throwing it back at her friend.

"I choose Charlie."

"Oh like we didn't see that coming from a mile away," Donna said with a roll of her eyes. "Mindy, why don't you just ask him out?"

"Because thanks to Rebecca, I'm invisible."

"That's not true!"

"It's kinda true," Donna offered. "He's still pining for you, Beccs."

"I know, and I'm going to talk to him when he gets back," Rebecca replied, cursing herself for not having ended it earlier.

"The current situation isn't helping matters either. It's the whole damsel in distress thing."

"Hey, I'm a damsel in distress," Mindy said as she perked up.

"Leave it alone, trust me you don't want to go there."

"So that leaves Detective Eric," Donna said as she met Rebecca's hesitant eyes.

"No, it really doesn't."

"Why?"

"It's complicated," Rebecca replied as she wiped down the counter.

"No it's not, you're just making it complicated and I'd really like to know why."

She kept telling herself it was complicated, but the truth was, it wasn't. Eric Stiles had stolen her heart long before she ever knew his name.

"Yeah what's up with that? Besides the fact that he's Charlie's brother and a definite no-no," Mindy started questioning her. "You haven't even broken up with Charlie yet and you . . ."

"Don't you think I know that, Mindy?" Rebecca snapped, her frustration getting the better of her as her body started to tremble. "For the millionth time, there is nothing going on between Eric and me! Would it be too much to ask you to stop shoving him in my face as if he were some piece of meat? I'm breaking up with Charlie! Go for it, he's all yours, just stay out of my love life, okay?"

"Beccs, I didn't mean—"

"I know, I just . . . I can't deal with all of this right now."

"It's okay, you're going through a lot," Donna offered as she wrapped her arms around her shoulders. "You don't need to decide anything or be put under any more pressure."

"I'm sorry, Beccs. I was just teasing, sort of," Mindy offered as she wrapped her arms around Rebecca's waist and they had a group hug. "We're going to get through this, all of us."

"I love you, guys," Rebecca said as she hugged them both. "We love you, too."

Mike opened the door with his free hand and Eric followed him into the house his arms full of Chinese food. Glancing into the house, he caught sight of the three women parting from what looked like a group hug. Rebecca remained at the sink with her back to him and then she turned around, facing them with a grin.

"What took you guys so long?" she asked.

He began unloading the bags onto the counter. He tried to catch her eye, but for whatever reason, she seemed to be avoiding his gaze.

They dished out the food and were all sitting around Rebecca's dining room table, eating and talking.

"So Eric, do you like being a cop?" Mike asked as Mindy elbowed him.

"It has its moments like any other job," he said, glancing as Rebecca got up from the table and walked into the kitchen.

"It's pretty dangerous though, that's gotta suck," Mindy commented.

"I'm trained to handle the risks associated with the job," he replied with a small grin as if he were used to the questions. "But yeah, it's still hard."

"Well thanks for all that you do for the city," Mike said with a nod.

Eric grinned as he rose from his seat and moved into the kitchen. She was doing the dishes and he grabbed a towel off the counter. "Can I help?" he asked.

She turned with a smile. "Yeah, that would be great," she replied. "You can start on those if you want. Just stack them on the island when you're done and I'll put them away."

Eric began drying dishes and there was an easy silence between them that he enjoyed. After a few moments, Mindy, Mike and Donna joined them in the kitchen, each of them taking a task to assist in the cleanup. Eric was reaching for the last of the plates as Donna whipped a towel at Mike. He howled in a high-pitched tone and the room erupted into laughter. Feeling his phone vibrating against his hip, Eric set the towel on the counter and pulled it out. There was a message from Adam waiting and Eric stepped away to listen to the voicemail.

They needed him down at the station. Eric put away his phone as he looked at Rebecca and realized her eyes were already on him. He held them for a moment as the calmness that had settled over him whined in protest.

She broke the gaze, looking away from him as if it was too painful to continue.

"Well folks, it's been fun, but work calls," Eric announced to the room as Rebecca pushed her hand through her hair and headed to the door. Donna, Mindy and Mike said their goodbyes and Eric met her at the door, her eyes glistening against the moonlight.

"I'm glad you stayed."

"So am I," he replied with a smile, shoving his hands in his pockets as he tried to hide the sudden need to touch her.

"So I guess I'll see you at the bar?"

"Yeah, Charlie will be home in a few days and we usually have a party," he replied, the swell in his chest deflating a little.

"Let me know when and where and we'll be there."

"Have a good night, Beccs," he said, dipping his head as he forced himself out the door.

"You, too," she replied.

He turned back, seeing a genuine unease in her eyes.

"Be safe, Eric."

"I will," he replied, giving her a small smirk in reassurance. Eric walked to the truck, not wanting to look back for fear of never leaving. He heard the door close behind him and getting in the truck, he took a breath and headed to the station.

Someone had just made coffee, so Eric grabbed his cup off the desk, desperate for a pick-me-up. He opened the fridge and realized there was no cream. His head fell to his chest as he walked away. No cream, no coffee. He couldn't drink it black.

Crap.

He dug in his pockets for change and stopped, feeling something unfamiliar. He pulled it out and saw two twenties. He was confused for a moment and then realized Rebecca must have slipped them into his jacket when he wasn't looking.

He couldn't help but smirk as he remembered a few random moments from the day. He headed to the vending machine and popped a dollar worth of quarters into the machine. He hit the Coke button. Hearing the machine pop, Eric felt his cell buzz. He pulled it out and looked at it as he grabbed his Coke. Seeing Rebecca's name, he opened the message, reading it.

You left your sunglasses on my counter.

He grinned at the message and typed a message back.

You left two twenties in my pocket.

Eric put the phone away and headed to his desk. He figured she was asleep and it was an old message. When the phone vibrated again, he pulled it out in surprise.

Don't you love it when you find money in your pocket?
Good, then you'll be excited when they show up in your pocket.
Don't start a money war with me, Stiles, you'll lose,
Uh huh. Shouldn't you be sleeping?

Shouldn't you?

I'm working, what's your excuse?

No excuse, just couldn't sleep so I decided to quit trying.

Debating his response, he sat back and stared down at the blank screen.

Beccs, you need to sleep.

I'm thinking I need a run.

His stomach dropped and he forced himself to not over-react. She didn't need to be going on a run, alone, in the dark, at three forty-five in the morning.

Please don't.

Eric tried not to stare at the phone as he waited for a response. After a few minutes, he got anxious and annoyed with her.

Beccs?

He waited and the phone buzzed in his hand.

Fine, I'll wait until Donna wakes up. Tom & Jerry is on anyway.

Thank you.

He hit send and exhaled a relieved breath, putting the phone aside as he booted up his computer.

Chapter Fifteen

The next three days flew by like a nightmare. Work flared up again, but Rebecca's admirer had decided to take a break. Eric traded text messages back and forth with her over the course. He found it amazing how she knew the perfect moments to begin their electronic banter. It was always when she was on his mind or he needed a distraction from the ugliness of his job.

"God, I'm starving," Adam declared as he looked at his watch. "I'm hitting the vending machine, do you want anything?"

"I'm good, thanks," Eric said as he dialed into his voicemail. Deleting as he went, he got to the last message and heard Charlie's voice. Listening to the jovial message about his return, Eric felt a lead weight drop into his stomach. Deleting the message, he tossed his phone on the desk and rubbed his eyes as they burned with fatigue.

He was glad his brother was home safe, but the sinking heaviness continued as he thought of Rebecca. The easiness that had developed in the few days and hours they'd spent together was going to disappear. Charlie was his brother. As long as he was interested in Rebecca, he needed to back off, despite his own feelings. He had a sense that she knew that as well. Which explained why she'd tried to keep her distance from him.

Adam returned with a pile of junk food.

Eric pushed the ache in his chest aside and dove head first into his work.

Work would make it all go away.
Work would make it better.

"Don, are you ready?" Rebecca called into the apartment as she switched her needed items into a bar purse she borrowed from her. Despite her window being fixed, Eric insisted that she stay with Donna. Things seemed to have settled down, but she wasn't sure if the reason was her change of location.

Maybe it was over . . .

"Yeah, sorry," she said as she appeared beside her. "I was on the phone with my mom."

"Good thing we're going to get a drink," Rebecca commented with a smirk as Donna locked the door behind them and they got in the car to pick up Mindy.

"I swear to the heavens, does she not realize that it's my biological clock and I can hear it just fine without her?"

"Is she on the grandkid kick again?"

"Her friend Patty just welcomed her sixth," Donna commented as she pulled down the mirror and began to apply her mascara. "It's so bad that she's even dropping hints about artificial insemination."

"Seriously?"

"I'm so not kidding," Donna replied with a nod as she put her makeup away and then looked at her with a smirk.

"What?"

"So, I know I may be treading on thin ice, but what's the real story between you and Eric?"

"What do you mean?"

"Beccs, you can't tell me that there's nothing going on between you and our handsome detective," she replied with the utmost sincerity. "The electricity in the room anytime you two are together is absolutely magnetic!"

"Where do you get this stuff, Don?"

"I'm sorry, I can't help it, I just pick up on things," she replied with a shrug,

Rebecca could feel her perceptive eyes boring into her.

"So, you're not denying it."

Rebecca looked at her as she drove, debating about whether or not to tell her the truth. Would it hurt anything? If anything, she would have someone to use as a sounding board which was something she missed.

She was tired of arguing with herself. She'd much rather argue with someone else about the chaotic mess her life had become. Making the decision, she found a parking lot, pulled off and stopped the car.

"What is it?"

"There's something I haven't told you," Rebecca confessed as she rested her cheek against the steering wheel, looking at her friend's expectant eyes. "I met Eric in Dallas."

"In Dallas, when?"

"On my way back from getting Lucy."

"How?"

"My flight got cancelled because of a storm in Chicago. I got a hotel room, there was a bar and I decided to make some money," she explained before taking a deep breath as the night replayed in her mind.

"You found a pool table then?" Donna asked and Rebecca nodded. "How much did you make?"

"Four-fifty."

"Good night, Beccs."

"It wasn't fair, they were all drunk."

"Okay, back to the story. So you were down at the bar playing pool . . ."

"At the end of my last game, I looked up and he was just there, watching," she explained, remembering the relaxed look on his face. "I dismissed it and went out for a cigarette. When I came back, he was at the bar with a perky blonde."

"Fun, did you squash her?"

"Not quite," Rebecca replied with a smirk. "I was standing behind her at the bar and he saw me. So he was talking to her, but looking at me, like he was talking to me."

"Interesting, then what?"

"I think Mindy called and I went outside to talk to her," she replied. "When I came back inside, he was in the lobby and I asked him if he wanted to get a coffee and he said yes."

"So you had coffee and that was it?"

"Oh no, that would be too easy," Rebecca replied as she leaned back in her seat, staring at the ceiling. "I tried to be good, I really did."

"Enough, tell me."

"We went for coffee, had a nice time and we made a deal at the coffee shop that we were going to keep everything in generalities, no names and no personal stuff. We both knew, or thought, that we would never see each other again so why get personal, right?"

"Very logical."

"So we walked back from coffee and I said good night and went up to my room," Rebecca continued. "I stopped by the vending machine to get some water . . ."

"Two water and two aspirin . . ."

"Exactly," Rebecca nodded as she came to the part of the story that made her heart ache and her stomach do flip-flops. "So I'm walking back to my room and he comes walking around the corner."

"He followed you?"

"No, his room was across the hall from mine."

"No way," Donna replied with a giggle.

Rebecca rolled her eyes at the drama.

"What are the freaking odds?"

"So I'm standing there, bottles of water in my hand and

he just walks up and plants this . . . this amazing kiss on me. I don't know if it was the alcohol or my frame of mind or if he's just a really good kisser, but, Donna, I lost it. The next thing I know, we're in his room and . . ."

"You slept with him," Donna said as a confirmation.

Rebecca nodded before lowering her forehead onto the steering wheel in defeat.

"Oh dear. Wow, Beccs, that's a doozie."

All she could do was whimper as she relived him making love to her and the heat of his touch, the softness of his lips.

"So wait, when Charlie introduced you that night at the police station, neither of you had any idea that . . ."

"None," Rebecca replied as she sat back, running her fingers through her hair.

"So have you and Eric talked about it? What did he say when—"

"Nothing."

"Nothing?"

"Nothing. We haven't spoken of it, not out loud anyway."

"So you've both been carrying this around this whole time?" Donna replied in shock. "And Charlie has no idea."

"Not that I know of."

"So I'm going to assume that the problem here is not a one night stand?"

"I've tried to ignore it, to ignore him, but ever since that night," she began to explain as she picked at her steering wheel. "Even before I knew who he was, I haven't been able to stop thinking about him."

"And now that you've seen him again, it's only gotten worse?"

"Bingo," Rebecca replied in irritation with her own weakness. "But how can I trust any of it, Don? I'm not exactly in the most stable frame of mind right now. What if I just think I'm attracted to him because of the whole damsel in distress thing you said the other night?"

"Rebecca, that's not what this is."

"How do you know?"

"I know," Donna reassured her. "If anything, the fact that you're continuing to have these feelings for him amidst all of this chaos shows just how strong those feelings are. I know that all of this is coming at the exact wrong time, and the circumstances suck, but you need to ride it out and let it lay. Everything happens for a reason, and there's a reason he's come into your life at this moment in time. Trust me, it'll work itself out."

Rebecca couldn't help but laugh aloud at Donna's sage wisdom as her phone buzzed. "Do you lay awake at night and think this shit up?"

"Sometimes, yes . . ." Donna replied.

It sent Rebecca into another fit of giggles as she looked at her phone.

"Is that Mindy?"

"Yeah, she's going to kill me," Rebecca said as she restarted the car and pulled back onto the road.

"I'll take the heat for it, don't worry," Donna said as she shifted back into her seat.

"What are you going to say?"

"I'll think of something," Donna replied with a wide grin and then squeezed Rebecca's hand in reassurance. "It's gonna be okay."

Chapter Sixteen

Eric opened the door to the bar, blasted by smoke, music and laughter. The place was packed and he had to push his way through the crowd to the bar. The bar staff was busy, so he reached across and grabbed a beer out of the cooler.

"You're gonna pay for that, right?"

"I've got an in with the owner," Eric replied as he reached out his hand, pulling Charlie into a man hug. "Are you in one piece?"

"As far as I know. You never know what I might find later though."

"Yeah right," Eric laughed and they both heard a corner of the bar roar. "What's going on over there?"

"Beccs is kickin' some guy's ass at pool," Charlie replied, his eyes gleaming in happiness. "Last time I checked, the pot was up to 200."

"Nice," Eric replied, careful not to show any unneeded interest.

"So, I haven't had a chance to talk to her yet. How did everything go while I was gone?" Charlie asked.

Eric's mind drifted to her smile. "It was pretty quiet, there were a few little things, but overall, it was fine."

"A few little things, what does that mean?"

"Ah . . . you should probably ask Rebecca."

"She's going to tell me everything is fine like she always does," Charlie replied in mild irritation as he looked over to the crowd surrounding the pool tables.

Eric focused on the bottle in front of him.

"Thus the reason I'm asking you."

"Rebecca will tell you what she wants to tell you," Eric replied, smirking to try and cover the irritation in his voice. "The only thing I can tell you is that she's safe and we handled anything that may have happened."

"Any clues as to who is doing this to her?"

"Not yet, but they're working on it."

There was another whooping cheer.

While Eric was tempted to go and watch her in action, he decided instead to down his beer and order another. Finishing the one in his hand, he heard a rumble at the door and the familiar calling of his name as his buddies, Don and Jerry, walked into the bar.

The men caught up on the latest events and then headed to the dartboard. Eric was killing them and the time flew. He heard the tapping of the sound system and turned to see a band getting ready to start. Charlie introduced them to the crowd as the Regals and the band started their set. Eric turned back to the darts and caught sight of Rebecca standing at the bar, laughing at something Donna said. His heart lifted at the joy in her face and he forced himself to turn away.

They finished their game of darts and Jerry suggested they move on to pool. He moved toward the table and began racking the balls when Donna and Mindy appeared at the corner of the table.

"Can we help you, ladies?" Don asked as Eric began to chalk his cue.

"You're playing on our table," Mindy said sassily.

Eric smirked. "Your table?"

"Yeah, our table. Ever hear of a marker?" Donna replied as she lifted a black tab attached to the side of the table.

"No, actually we haven't," Jerry replied with a laugh as

he looked over Donna with a smile. "Sorry, we have dibbs, plus Eric is the owner's brother which trumps your marker."

"Okay, how about we play you for it," Donna offered as the men looked at each other and then Eric.

"Don't look at me, you guys are the ones who wanted to play pool," he replied, leaning against the wall, crossing his arms in amusement.

"Deal. Jerry, you're sitting this one out," Don stated as the girls proceeded to pick their cues off the wall.

"No need," Rebecca said as she joined the group.

Her eyes were almost shining just as they had the first night Eric had found himself captivated by her.

"We can all play."

The game began with Eric breaking the rack and choosing solids. Overall the teams were evenly matched, Eric and Rebecca being the strongest players on each team. Eric had done his best to keep her at bay, but she beat him and the girls won the table. The group decided to keep playing together despite the agreement and a round of beers was ordered.

Eric kept to one side of the table and Rebecca stayed on the other. Anytime their bodies came into proximity, one of them would move. It was an unspoken agreement and yet Eric found it annoying. It was everything he could do to stay away from her, seeking even the slightest brush as a squelching to the fire that raged within him.

He focused on the game as his shot came up. Concentrating, he heard the bar waitress behind him and Rebecca said something in return. Taking the shot, he followed the path of the ball and turned to call the next shot. As he turned, he heard a yelp and saw Rebecca in front of him, a tray of drinks wobbling in her hands. He grabbed the sides of the tray to help steady it and wound up covering her hands with his own. His eyes lifted, looking at her as she stared at the tray in her hands with hesitation. "Got it?" he asked.

She met his gaze with a smirk of embarrassment. "Yeah, I think so," she replied as the tray began to wobble again.

"Are you sure because if I let go and you dump it down the front of me, we're going to have a problem."

"Why, did you spend a whole twenty dollars on your shirt?" she replied as she attempted to steady the tray with a giggle.

"No," he replied with a small chuckle at the comment as he kept his hands on the tray, helping her to steady it as the bottles clinked together. "It's my last clean shirt."

"Stop making me laugh!"

"Stop threatening to spill beer all over me!"

They settled the beers on the tray and Eric looked at her as he let go of the tray and she held it steady. She smiled at him with a nod as he raised his arms out of the way and stepped aside to let her pass. Watching her carry the tray, she placed it on the table and he saw her laugh as Mindy made a comment to her.

"Eric, you going to shoot or what?"

The air in the room seemed to lighten a little, and he found himself bantering with Rebecca, Donna and the rest of the group. It was relaxed and he realized he'd become too relaxed when Charlie joined the group. Eric found himself having to find a distraction and focused on the game as Charlie brushed her hair off her shoulder or wrapped his arm around her back. The only consolation Eric found was that Rebecca seemed to be as bothered by his brother's affection as he was. Eric watched as she made every attempt to keep some distance between herself and Charlie.

The band was in the middle of their last set and starting the opening of a slow ballad. Eric heard Rebecca protest as Charlie pulled her toward the dance floor. He watched as she continued to object, but Charlie won out. Charlie's hands wrapped around her waist. Eric was finding it more and more difficult to contain the jealousy that filled his gut. He forced himself to turn away. He searched for a distraction and decided to follow the rest of the group to the bar.

"Mindy and I were debating a shot, would you like to join us?" Donna asked him with a knowing grin as he approached the bar.

"Sure, why not?" Eric replied with a shrug as he took a seat beside them.

"Charlie, I really don't want to dance."

"Please, Beccs?"

"Charlie . . ."

"Please, Beccs," he repeated, giving her the saddest puppy dog eyes.

She relented and moved with him onto the dance floor. He wrapped his hands around her waist as her hands rested on his shoulders. His warm gold-green eyes were full of expectation and her heart sank, knowing that she could never give him what he wanted from her.

"So Eric said things were okay while I was gone?"

"Yeah, everything was fine," she lied, conscious of the surrounding eyes on them. "I told you there was nothing to worry about."

"I know, but I can't help but worry about you, Beccs," he said as he pulled her closer.

She moved her hand to the center of his chest, creating a physical barrier between them.

"I really missed you."

"I missed you, too. It's always hard when one of my best friends is gone."

She wasn't sure if he understood what she was trying to say or not, but as she continued to keep his gaze, she felt his hand brush her hair. She realized what was going to happen and pulled back from him.

"Charlie," she said, pleading with him to hear her. His eyes turned from light and hopeful to clouded and confused and she anticipated his reaction. "I can't . . . I can't do this anymore. I'm sorry. I adore you as a friend, but this . . . I can't do this anymore."

He nodded and looked at her in regret before he pulled her into a hug against his chest.

She hugged him back and she felt him kiss the top of her head as the song ended. Rebecca stepped out of his embrace and made an excuse that she needed to use the ladies room. She moved across the bar to the ladies room, opened the door and found a barrage of people.

Oh hell no . . .

Deciding she'd had enough for one night, Rebecca looked at her watch and saw it was almost one AM.

They'd stayed long enough, time to hit the road. Rebecca squared her shoulders and walked back into the bar, seeing Donna and Mindy waving her over. Pushing her way through the crowd, she was happy to see that neither Charlie nor Eric were anywhere in sight.

"You ready to hit the road?"

"Read my mind."

"Let's go," Mindy finished as the women gathered their things, said some quick goodbyes, including a wave to the boys playing pool. Rebecca caught Eric's eye before he looked away and then went to say goodbye to Charlie. She moved toward him with a smile and he wrapped his arms around her.

"Love you, Beccs," he whispered.

She looked back at him with a small smile and laid a kiss on his cheek.

Her smile lit up the room as waves of fire rolled down her back. He waited, nursing his drink of choice until the opportunity arose. When it did, he was tender as he loaded her into the back of his yellow 1974 Volkswagen beetle. He had the perfect place selected for their union. He laid her out on the bed and looked at his watch. He had five minutes to finish the preparations before she would wake. He finished lighting the candles and then laid out his tools on the dresser. He heard her begin to shift with soft coos and mumbling questions. He reclined on the bed next to her, ready to ease her fears when her eyes opened. She turned her head and looked at him with a heavy gaze. He smiled as he brushed the hair off her cheek.

"Welcome back, my love," he said as she sighed. His fingertips traced the crease of her neck as her eyes closed. He shifted and nibbled on the line of her chin as she began to roll beneath him. His threaded his fingers into her sensual hair and then he stopped. "No."

His eyes lifted as he pulled her hair through his hand. It felt synthetic and a deep growl erupted from his chest. He sat up and yanked at her hair. It ripped off her head, revealing her sunshine locks.

"No, no . . . no!" he yelled as he jumped off the bed. His plans for the evening disintegrated and the fragile shell of control shattered. He looked for resolution and lifted his skinning knife from the dresser. He turned, recalculating the steps of his expulsion as he stepped toward the bed.

She was rolling on the bed, her body warm in anticipation. The internal adjustment to his plans was complete, and he smiled in success. He knelt on the bed as he flipped her onto her stomach. He straddled her waist and gathered her blonde hair into his hands. It was soft like nylon, and he pulled. Her head lifted off the bed and bent backward toward his chest. She remained silent, ignorant of his plans.

He trapped her arms beneath his legs, as he leaned forward, pressing the knife into the peak of her forehead. Human skin was thicker than it appeared, and the first strip of her scalp cut like a shaving of moist cheese. Thankfully, he always sharpened his tools before he left the house.

He was immune to her screams of agony as he began on the second strip. He knew she would scream herself into unconsciousness soon enough. He started again at the top of her forehead, slid across the bone of her skull and stopped at the base of her neck. He continued his work as her wails ceased. He hummed Tchaikovsky as his thoughts hovered around his Aurora.

The light in his Aurora's eyes had dimmed and he regretted the next steps of the agenda. The power had been taken from his hands. His creative control remained steadfast, but the frequency and the extent of the messages was being administered elsewhere.

He relished the day when it would end and she would lay peaceful. Until then the deeds of the wicked must push forth as every moment passed was a moment wasted.

Chapter Seventeen

Rebecca shifted onto her back, her arm resting above her head as she stared at the ceiling. It was a nice ceiling, one of the more interesting ones she'd seen. However, the subtle waves and patterns couldn't pull the images from her head or stop her mind from running in circles.

She wanted to sleep, to fall into a deep dreamless sleep where she could forget every painful moment she'd experienced.

She tossed and turned for several hours and then looking at the clock, decided it was time to get up. She went into the kitchen for coffee and walked out onto the porch. Breathing in the cool desert air, she was out there for about half an hour when heard the door open.

"Hey," Donna greeted as she stepped out with smile.

"Hey."

"Did you get some sleep?" Donna asked.

Rebecca rolled her eyes and took a sip of her coffee.

"I'll take that as a no. Okay, sweetie. Sorry I have to bail, but I have an early meeting. Charlie should be here any minute. Try and rest, I'll call you later."

Rebecca nodded with a smile as Donna headed down the stairs and off to work. She stayed outside for another ten minutes and then headed in. She locked the door and put the coffee on the table as she flipped on the TV.

She heard her phone beeping from across the room and moved, pulling her purse off the chair as she dug for it. Finding it, she saw a waiting voicemail and she dialed in, hearing the haunting horrible garbled voice from the prank calls

Knock knock.

Who's there?

Donna.

Donna who?

Donna turn around, Ka- BOOM!

Rebecca panicked and then heard someone at the door.

"Beccs, are you there, it's me," Charlie called.

Rebecca grabbed her purse and dashed for the door. "We have to go!" she said as she opened the door and pushed him out.

"What, why?"

"Donna, he's going after Donna!"

"How do you . . ."

"There's no time, Charlie, we have to get to her before something happens!"

"Fine let's go," he said as they ran down the stairs and he dialed his phone.

Eric managed to get a few hours sleep in the cage before he was needed back in the bullpen. He was finding it more and more difficult to push her out of his mind. He went to get some coffee.

"Stiles," Lug said, breaking through his churning thoughts.

"Hey, what's up?" he replied as he grabbed his full cup of coffee.

"Trace on the box of blood came back," Lug said.

Eric walked to his desk. "And?"

"They found a piece of hair in the box sealant."

"Were they able to get a name?"

"Yeah," Lugow started as he looked down at his desk in hesitation. "It came as a match to a Veronica Naltin."

Eric froze as the name hit him in the chest. "What?"

"Yeah," Lug replied as Eric took a deep breath. "We double checked. There's no mistake."

"Jesus," Eric said as he leaned on the desk, his mind spinning uncontrolled.

Adam appeared and looked at him. "You told him?"

"Yeah."

"So now what?" Eric asked as he tried to reign in the fear that began to bubble in his stomach. They were not only dealing with a stalker, but now a ruthless killer.

"We start from the beginning," Adam said as Lug nodded. "We look at everything from both cases."

"We should look at anything that's happened since this guy made first contact with Rebecca," Lug suggested.

"Do we have a date?"

"The only specific date I have is two weeks before the teddy bear," Lug replied as he looked at his notes. "I will try and get something more specific."

"Where is she now?"

"Donna's," he said with a deep breath.

"Is she going to be safe there?"

"She'll be fine for now," Lugow added.

"Okay, let's get to work," Adam said.

Eric's phone rang. "Detective Stiles."

"Eric, we have a problem," Charlie said, sounding panicked and out of breath.

"What's going on?" he said, looking to Lug and Adam.

"Rebecca got a message from the stalker."

"When?"

"I little while ago," he replied.

Eric's heart began to race.

"We think he's going after Donna."

"Why?"

"I don't know. Something about the message."

"Did you hear it?"

"No."

"Let me talk to Rebecca," he said and then heard Charlie pass the phone to Rebecca.

"Eric," she said, sounding terrified and shaken.

Eric got to his feet as Adam followed him. "What did he say?"

"Uh, it was a joke."

"A what?"

"A knock, knock, joke."

"Tell me exactly what he said, Beccs."

"Knock, knock, who's there, Donna, Donna who, Donna turn around ka-boom," she said into the phone.

He could hear the agony in her voice. "Where are you?"

"On our way to Donna's office."

"Okay, let me talk to Charlie," he replied in an even tone. He heard her pass the phone back to Charlie.

"Hey," Charlie said.

Eric and Adam reached Adam's car. "Have either of you tried to call her yet?"

"Yeah, she's not answering, but Beccs said she had an early meeting."

"We're on our way to Donna's office as well, but you need to stall and keep Rebecca away until I tell you it's okay."

"That's going to be pretty hard to do."

"Listen to me, this could all be a way to lure Rebecca out into the open," Eric explained as Adam pulled onto the street. "Just stall long enough for us to make sure it's safe."

"Okay," Charlie agreed before Eric hung up.

"What's going on?" Adam asked.

"Rebecca got a message from the stalker."

"What kind of message?"

"One with a ka-boom."

Eric, Adam, Lug and the bomb squad arrived in front of Donna's office twenty minutes later. Adam coordinated the sweep and evacuation of the building while Eric went looking for Donna. He stepped off the elevator and flashed his badge to the receptionist. "Detective Stiles, I need to speak with Donna Smith, it's an emergency," Eric said as the woman looked at him in confusion.

"I thought you were meeting her in the parking garage," the woman replied.

Eric spun, dashing to the elevator as he called Adam. "She was called down to the parking garage, I'm on my way now," Eric said into the phone hitting the *P* on the elevator. The doors opened moments later, and as he stepped off, he saw Donna leaning against her car with a look of irritation. "Donna!" he called out to her.

She shifted, looking.

He ran toward her.

"Eric, what's going on?" she asked as she moved to meet him.

Eric heard a door slam just to the left.

"Is Beccs alright?"

"She got a call from the stalker. He . . ."

"Donna!" Rebecca called as she ran toward them, Charlie in tow.

He realized that Rebecca was going to pass right in front of Donna's car. "Beccs, *no!*" he screamed, pushing Donna behind him just before the car exploded. The blast pushed both he and Donna off their feet as it shattered and sprayed glass across the parking lot. Eric recovered and bolted upright to see Rebecca and Charlie flat on the ground, Charlie covering her with his body. He waited for a moment.

They moved, looking at him in breathless shock.

Eric forced his lungs to inhale air, begging his heart to restart as Rebecca and Charlie crossed the area to meet them.

Rebecca said nothing and ran toward them, trembling. She wrapped herself around Donna and Charlie looked at Eric in regret.

"I thought I told you to keep her away from here," Eric said in a low tone as he pulled Charlie off to the side.

"I tried, but she . . ." Charlie tried to defend.

Eric rubbed his neck, turning away.

"What the hell was that, a concussion grenade?"

"I . . . I'm fine," Donna replied looking at Eric as she hugged Rebecca.

"Yeah, looks like it," Eric said as he stared at the car while trying to subdue his welling irritation and rage.

"I'm so sorry, Don . . . I didn't . . ."

"It's okay. I'm okay, Beccs," Donna reassured as the cavalry in the form of Adam and the bomb squad arrived. "So much for my morning meeting."

Chapter Eighteen

"Says the tip came from apartment 508," Adam said as they entered the five-story apartment complex and both noticed the out-of-service elevator sitting in front of them.

An anonymous tip, claiming to be a concerned citizen, came in, stating that they would find something interesting on the fifth floor of the building.

"Of course it did."

The remnants of Donna's car and the bomb that destroyed it offered no assistance. Donna, Rebecca and Charlie gave their statements and were home hours later. Two days had passed and Eric was on edge. If their stalker kept to his current schedule, they should be expecting something. Lug knew it as well and he had his entire team on alert. When this new tip came in, they offered to check it out.

They reached the fifth floor, not too winded, and found the apartment number. They knocked on the door and it swung open.

"LVPD, anyone home?" Adam called into the apartment as he looked in.

Eric stepped into the doorway as well, scanning the room. He saw something around the corner and craned his neck to see. "Can you see around that corner?"

"Where?"

"Over here on my right," Eric replied.

Adam leaned forward, looked at Eric and nodded. "We have probable cause, let's go."

They entered the apartment, turned to the right corner

and were faced with a wall of photos. All of Rebecca and Lucy Gailen.

"We need to call Lug," Adam said as he dialed his phone.

The crashing of glass erupted from the next room and seeing movement out of the corner of his eye, Eric darted after it. *"Runner!"* Eric tore through the apartment and entered the back bedroom just as a male suspect was trying to escape out the window.

"Stop! Police!"

The suspect turned and fired.

Eric fired back. A searing heat sliced through his left arm. The bullet hit the suspect in the leg, with a minor flesh wound. Eric kicked the gun out of the suspect's hand. Adam rushed the room and grabbed the discarded weapon. Eric grasped the man by the collar and hauled him back. He pushed him against the wall and handcuffed him while reading him his rights. "Call a bus," Eric said as he turned the suspect around to face him. "What's your name?"

"Ken!"

"Ken? Have a seat," Eric shoved the man to the floor. "Don't move."

"Pigs . . ." the suspect replied.

Eric ignored him. Eric stepped back and holstered his weapon as a shooting pain rose up his arm to his shoulder. Looking over his arm in confusion, he saw his shirt covered in blood. "Crap."

"Are you okay?"

"Yeah, just let me find something to stop the bleeding," Eric said as he moved out of the room, leaving Adam to deal with their suspect. Eric walked through the apartment and found the kitchen. He searched for a clean towel. He pulled open drawers one at a time until he found one and pressed it to his arm with a wince of pain. He leaned against the counter, cursing his inability to move faster. His gaze moved to the corner of the kitchen, seeing two large white paint buckets. Moving toward them, he kicked one, seeing a rim of red around the bottom.

Paint?

Eric leaned over and smeared a finger through the red liquid. The smell of iron hit his senses and his stomach turned. He rose and turned to face the wall covered with photos of Rebecca and Lucy. He stepped closer as he gulped back the bile that began to pool in the back of his throat. Still shots of her from everywhere, her house, her work, the bar, the grocery store, it went on and on. "So Ken, how about you tell me a little about your wall over here?"

"That's not my wall."

"No, then whose is it?" Eric asked, receiving silence in response. "What about the buckets in the kitchen? Whose are those?" Eric then heard a thundering from the hall as their backup and the medical team arrived. "Adam," Eric called as he rose out of the way for the medical team.

"Yeah?"

"Take a look at this," Eric said as he led Adam into the kitchen.

Adam saw the buckets and repeated the same process. "Blood?"

"That was my thought."

"Jesus, there's got to be at least eight to ten gallons here. Looks like we are on the right track. What do you think about our friend?"

"He's not our guy, but he knows who is. Let the paramedics patch him up so we can have a chat," Eric replied. Sticky warmth slid down his arm.

"He's not the only one who needs to be patched up," Adam commented as he looked at his partner. "I'll let Lug know we'll meet him at the hospital."

She opened the door and was faced with a room filled with burned faces staring back at her, Lucy, Mindy, Donna, Mike, Charlie, her mother . . . they were reaching for her. She stepped back in fear, feeling warm arms around her. She leaned back into them, wanting him to tell her it was going to be okay. Instead, his grip on her became tighter, crushing her within his grasp. Bloody hands moved over her body. They turned her around and she was facing Marco. His face twisted, bruised and bloody. He smiled at her and then nuzzled her neck as the blood smeared her face.

"I want you so badly, Beccs," he said as he pushed her back.

She landed on a bed. He fell on top of her and she tried pushing him off, but he wouldn't move. She could feel him against her and she cried out. "Please . . ." she tried to scream, but the words came out as weak whispers. "Please stop . . ."

She heard a bang and Marco was pushed off her. Opening her eyes, she saw Eric's horrified expression staring down at her broken body. He was covered in blood, his face torn and dirty as he looked at her in anguish . . .

"Beccs . . . why . . . what have you done?"

Rebecca sat up, hearing herself screaming.

"Beccs . . ."

Turning, she saw Charlie.

"Are you okay?"

"Yeah," she replied still breathless as the images continued to scar her mind. "Yeah, I'm okay."

"Are you sure?"

"Yeah, I'm good," she replied with a nod and smile as she ran her fingers through her hair. "Where are we?"

"Right now, on the side of the road. You scared the shit out of me."

"Sorry."

"I'm just kidding," he replied, shaking his head. "But seriously we're just outside of town. We should be at my place in about an hour."

Charlie had offered to drive Donna to Orange County, CA for a conference she needed to attend. He said they could make it a road trip and get out of town for the day. This suggestion had come just after Eric had called and she knew what they were attempting to do.

It had been two days.

It was time for another visit.

She refused to think about it and had convinced herself that by blocking the possibility out, it somehow disappeared. "Can we stop at the house first? I need to pick up my phone charger and my laptop," she requested as he pulled back onto the road. She tried to relax as the sun set.

"Yeah, okay."

She glanced at Charlie who seemed hesitant.

Rebecca could tell that something was on his mind, "Okay, let's have it."

"What?"

"Whatever it is that you're trying not to ask me."

"Am I really that transparent?"

"No, I have just gotten good at reading you. So talk to me."

"It can wait," he replied, keeping his eyes on the road.

"No, let's talk about it now. If I've learned anything, I need to stop procrastinating. So spill."

"Did I do something to ruin . . . us?"

"What? No, of course not, Charlie. I just . . ." she replied, trying to choose her words as she turned to face him. "My life is complicated right now. It isn't fair for me to ask you . . ."

"Rebecca, I want to be here, I care about you . . ."

"I know you do and you've been so wonderful through all of this. I truly adore and love you as a dear friend, but that's all. We just weren't meant to be." She watched him absorb her words.

He took a visible deep breath before he looked at her and

nodded. "I love you, Beccs," he started as he reached for her hand and squeezed it. "But I understand that all of this has got to be overwhelming."

"I'm so sorry, Charlie. I wish things could be different for us."

"So do I, but I want you to know that as your friend I'm not going anywhere. You don't have to go through this alone. I'm going to be right here to help you, no matter what."

"I don't deserve you, Charlie," she replied as she squeezed his hand. She wished she could give him what he wanted, but she couldn't. He was better off without her and she knew that.

"Yes you do, and more. You're going to get through this and it's going to work out, I promise."

Half an hour later, they arrived at Rebecca's house and the pair got out, walking toward it together.

"This will only take a minute. I need to grab a few things and then we can leave."

"Good, 'cause I'm going in first," he replied with a smile as he pushed her behind him.

The door whined as it opened.

Rebecca watched Charlie moved through the house and toward her bedroom. The house was still dark and she reached out, turning on the light. She thought about where she'd left her computer and what clothes she'd left at Donna's.

The room seemed darker and raising her eyes, they fell on the couch. All of the air disappeared as she tried to comprehend the scene laid out in her living room.

Her once cream-colored couch was now a deep crimson and bleeding onto the floor in front of her. Gasping for air, Rebecca stepped back, and her hand touched the wall for support.

"Looks okay," Charlie called as he stepped out of the bedroom in the area between the kitchen and the living room. "What's . . ."

The sound of his voice snapped her awake and she felt a sticky warmth slide on her palm. She focused on her hand and saw a crimson red as the smell of iron overwhelmed her senses. She saw nothing but blood red. It was smeared on the walls all around her. It cursed her with every stroke as the stench of it suffocated and horrified her in the same instant.

"Rebecca," Charlie said, his voice deep and terrified.

"Oh God . . ."

It was everywhere. There was no ignoring it or hiding from it. She tried to take a breath, but her lungs objected. Her legs wobbled and she reached out to steady herself. Something held her upright. She could hear a voice next to her, but there was no air. Nausea crept up into her throat as she looked at her hands again. She broke out of the warmth restricting her arms as she willed her legs to move.

She turned on the water as she reached the kitchen sink and shoved her hands beneath it while covering them in soap. She scrubbed the blood away. Her heart pounded in her ears as she heard someone's voice, in the distance. Her mind was distraught with the need to get it off. She had to get the blood off her hands.

It wouldn't come off and she scrubbed harder.

No . . . No . . . I have to get it off . . .

To Be Continued . . .

About the Author

Amy is a wife, mother of three and full time corporate employee. Amy has two dogs and a cat, enjoys movies, music and spending time with friends. Amy's writing heart beats to the fast paced, twisting, romantic thriller, but has also dabbled in theatre as an actress and director, written young adult romance and actively explored alternative venues for corporate marketing.

Amy works for a global document solutions company and current resides in Texas.

My Mantra

I believe Everything Happens for a Reason

I believe in True Love

I believe in Fate

I believe in Optimism

I believe in Imagination

I believe in Hard Work

I believe in Family